BRED BY THE SLUMS 2

Lock Down Publications and Ca$h
Presents
Bred by the Slums 2
A Novel by *Ghost*

Lock Down Publications

P.O. Box 870494
Mesquite, Tx 75187

Visit our website at www.lockdownpublications.com

Lock Down Publications
Like our page on Facebook: Lock Down Publications @
www.facebook.com/lockdownpublications.ldp
Cover design and layout by: **Dynasty Cover Me**
Book interior design by: **Shawn Walker**
Edited by: **Sunny Giovanni**

Stay Connected with Us!

Text **LOCKDOWN** to 22828 to stay
up-to-date with new releases, sneak peaks,
contests and more…

Submission Guideline.

Submit the first three chapters of your completed manuscript to ldpsubmissions@gmail.com, subject line: Your book's title. The manuscript must be in a .doc file and sent as an attachment. Document should be in Times New Roman, double spaced and in size 12 font. Also, provide your synopsis and full contact information. If sending multiple submissions, they must each be in a separate email.

Have a story but no way to send it electronically? You can still submit to LDP/Ca$h Presents. Send in the first three chapters, written or typed, of your completed manuscript to:

LDP: Submissions Dept
Po Box 870494
Mesquite, Tx 75187

DO NOT send original manuscript. Must be a duplicate.

Provide your synopsis and a cover letter containing your full contact information.

Thanks for considering LDP and Ca$h Presents.

DEDICATION

This book is dedicated to my precious, beautiful Baby girl. The love of my life, 3/10. Everything I do is for YOU, first and foremost.

ACKNOWLEDGEMENTS

I would like to thank the Boss Man and C.E.O of LDP, Cash. Thank you for this opportunity. Your wisdom, motivation and encouragement are appreciated. Thanks, Bruh.

To the Queen and C.O.O of LDP, thank you for all that you do Sis. Your hard work, dedication and loyalty to this company never goes unnoticed.

Ghost

Chapter 1

Chick-chick! Boom! The bullets from Mrs. Robinson's double barrel shotgun slammed into the wall in front of me and knocked a huge chunk of plaster right out of it. White smoke warped into the air, going into my mouth and causing me to choke. For a few seconds, I was blinded. The sirens from the police cars grew louder until I could hear them slam on their brakes out front. My heart was beating faster than an African drummer on steroids. I felt myself beginning to panic, and I couldn't control it.

Chick-chick! Boom! Another two big holes appeared in the wall, right along the side of my sister Purity's bedroom door. I had actually felt it whip past my ear. A little more to the left and my brains would have been all over the carpet in the Deacon's house.

"Son of a bitch! You killed my husband! You fuckin' killed him!" Mrs. Robinson screamed, before cocking the huge shotgun and pulling the trigger. *Click! Click! Click!* "Fuck!"

I looked over my shoulder in time to see her kneel with the big shotgun in her hands. She bussed it open, went into her bra, pulled out some red shelled bullets and started to reload the gun, all the while with tears running down her cheeks.

Though I was on the way to my sister's room, so I could jump back out of her window, I knew that I had to use her carelessness against her or it would wind up killing me later in more ways than one. So, I turned around and fell onto my back just as she snapped the shotgun closed and pumped it. She put the handle against her shoulder and got ready to aim, but I was way too quick, and way too scared to allow for that to happen.

The .45 was already out of the small of my back and in my hands. I aimed and let that bitch ride for all it was worth. *Boom! Boom! Boom! Boom! Boom! Boom!* The first bullet slammed into her chest and caused her to drop the shotgun with a look of shock on her face. The next few bullets hit her stomach, face, and all the rest went into her mid-section, punching holes into her center, before she fell to her knees and onto her face.

I jumped up and ran toward the back door. I could hear a bunch of footsteps on the front porch of her house, and I knew it had to be the police. There were three dead bodies in the house. The Deacon, his wife, and his oldest son, Mark. Both Mark and the Deacon had been raping my sister Purity for the last four months, and now at the age of sixteen she was forcibly pregnant by one of them, but she wasn't sure which.

Purity had been adopted by their family after our parents passed away from drug overdoses when we were just little kids. I was a day away from my eighteenth birthday, and I had spent the last year hustling and bussing major moves so I could get my sister out of foster care, when I became an adult. My main focus was on becoming financially stable, and to become that, I did whatever it took. I lived by the gun and I was pretty sure I was gon' die by it real soon.

I got to the back door of the Deacon's house, and unlocked it before throwing it open and running out into the backyard. Running like my life depended on it into the night. My book bag felt more heavy now on my shoulders.

I hopped the fence and came down on two feet, hit the alley and ran as fast as I could. It already felt like I was being stabbed in the chest with an ice sickle, but I had to get away from there. The Pastor and his wife only lived about a block away, and I was on my way there. After our parents passed away, I was adopted by the Pastor of our church and his wife. Though they were no longer together, I still lived with Vicki, which was the Pastor's wife, and their daughter, Simone.

More sirens sounded off into the distance. I knew they were headed for the Deacon's house and I was so glad that I was getting farther and farther away from there. I could only imagine what would take place once they found all of those bodies inside.

I felt my phone buzz again. I knew it was the Pastor's wife, who I now called my mother, trying to get in touch with me to keep me informed with updates on my right hand and best friend, Nikki, who had been gunned down in her trap house less than a week ago. She'd finally made it out of her coma, and was now calling for me to be by her side, which I intended to be as soon as I shook the current chaos that I was in.

"Huh. Huh. Huh." I muffled while I ran, then jumped the fence to our backyard, ran straight to the backdoor, went into my pocket and pulled out the key, letting myself in. As soon as I closed the door, I slid down it and sat there with my back against it, trying to catch my breath. I felt like I was going to throw up my heart or something.

Finally, after gathering myself a little bit, I got up and made my way into the house, and into the living room, stopping in front of the roaring fireplace and getting ass naked, throwing each article of clothing into it one by one, after making sure that there was nothing in the pockets. I watched the flames engulf them, then I jogged out of there, and into my room, grabbing some fresh boxers, black beater, and ankle socks, before going to the bathroom and showering. I had to get all of their blood off of me, just in case I was snatched by the police or something. I was in the game and I knew how shit went. Most niggas got caught down the road because of what they neglected to do, directly after their murders. Trust me, the next hour after killing somebody is always the most important one.

After showering, I rubbed my body down with rubbing alcohol, and then lotion. The alcohol would take any trace of blood off of me that the water did not, and the lotion sealed my sanitation and gave me a normal scent. I felt like I had done everything that I was supposed to do, now all that was left was to get rid of the knife and .45, which both would be broken down and thrown into the river.

Tap. Tap. Tap. Tap. I damn near jumped out of my skin at the sound of somebody knocking on the bathroom door. I was praying that it wasn't the police.

I ran the cold towel over my face again. "Who is it?" I asked, now putting my ear on the door.

"It's me— Simone. Are you okay in there? I'm worried about you."

I knew I had to play things cool. Like I said, the hour directly after your murder was always the most important one.

I took a deep breath and opened the door. There was Simone standing there in only a short purple night gown that barely fell below her cat. Both thighs were thick, caramel and shiny as if she'd just rubbed a gang of baby oil all over them. Her pretty face looked worried with a hint of concern.

"I'm good, baby. What's the matter with you?" I pulled her to me and wrapped my arms

around her small waist, kissing her on the neck, sucking loudly.

She moaned. "Umm-a. Shit, there you go already, Shemar. You always riling me up. Dang." She took a step back, then tilted her head so she could kiss my lips while she held the sides of my face, and I gripped that big ass booty. Even though Simone was a lil' younger than me, she was strapped like one of the coldest strippers here in Houston. On top of that, she was fine as hell.

I had a lil' thing for her ever since she'd given me her virginity. I gripped that ass and opened the cheeks. Even though I really wasn't in the mood to be fucking, I had to make everything seem like it was normal. Whenever me and her were alone, we were always getting it in on some level. I was addicted to her lil' body just like she was mine.

I pushed her up against the wall and bit into her neck, sliding my hands up her gown until I was cupping her titties, then sucking the nipples through the fabric. "You wanna give big bruh some of this pussy, don't you?"

She snaked her hand under her gown, and I peeped it moving around under there. I couldn't see exactly what she was doing, but I had an idea. "Unn-a." She threw her head back and moaned to the ceiling. "Yeah, Shemar. Can you? Unn-a. Can you give me a quickie real fast, from the back? I love when you fuck me from the back, and I need it so bad." She pulled her gown all the way up so I could watch her fingers rub in between her sex lips. She rubbed them up and down, real fast, before squeezing her lips together, causing a thick line of juice to drip down her thigh.

I could hear a whole bunch of sirens now, somewhere down the street. I imagined headed toward the Deacon's house, and I started to panic a lil' bit. My breathing became labored. I had to do something to take my mind off of what I was faced with.

Simone pushed me slightly in the chest, then marched over to the tub and bent over it, pulling her gown all the way up, exposing her ass cheeks. Then, she spread her legs, reached under herself and held her sex lips apart. "Come on, big bruh, put that big dick in me for a lil' while. I need it so bad." She sucked on her bottom lip, then slid two fingers into her hole, closing her eyes. "Umm." The fingers worked in and out of her in a rhythmic motion.

After seeing all of that, it was easy for me to put what I was going through out of my mind, if only for a short moment. I got behind her, stroking my dick, then placed the head at her pussy and pushed him in with force.

"Uhhh-a! Ummm-a! Shit! Fuck me, bruh! Fuck me hard, Shemar. You said you wasn't gon' play with my pussy no more because I'm ready now. So, don't. Please." She slammed her ass back into my lap.

I grabbed her hips and started to fuck her with all of my might. Hitting that shit hard like that pussy deserved. *Bam! Bam! Bam! Bam! Bam! Bam!* Her ass jiggled and shook, while her pussy walls sucked at me hungrily. Her titties bounced back and forth on her chest; the nipples standing erect.

Her heat felt so good that I couldn't help making noises. "Hmmm. Simone. Hmmm-uh. Hmmm-uh. Give me this pussy. Give me this shit. I'm finna kill this shit!" I got to fucking her so hard that she started screaming, and I didn't even care. I was too busy pulling her ass back to me again and again. It felt so good and hot. Her juices trailed to my balls and dripped off of them. The harder I hit that shit, the wetter she got.

Simone bent all the way over and kept on crashing back into me. I watched my dick go in and out of her sex lips, revealing her pink before shielding it again. "Shemar! Shemar! I'm cumming, Shemar! I'm cuminnnggggg!" She screamed and bounced her ass into my lap, over and over again, nice and hard.

As soon as she started to cum, I blasted off, biting into my bottom lip. My abs tightened, and the next thing I knew, I was letting loose, deep within her.

Afterward, she sat on the side of my bed while I got dressed. "My momma been calling my phone, trying to get into contact with you all night. She say Nikki out of her coma, and that she needs you." Simone kissed my stomach before I could button up my Polo shirt.

I had to laugh at that because she loved her some abs. "I just texted her and told her I was on my way over there, right now. If you wanna roll with me that's cool." I wanted to keep her as close to me as possible. That way, she could act as my alibi if I needed her to. I didn't know what was about to come my way, and I just wanted to be covered on all bases.

About ten minutes later, we stepped out of the house. I looked down the street and saw what looked like a hundred police cars on the block where the Deacon's house was. That gave me butterflies in my stomach.

Simone stopped in her tracks. "Dang, what happened down there?" She looked like she was about to walk off of the porch to investigate, and I surely wasn't finna allow that.

I grabbed her hand. "I don't know, but it ain't none of our business. Get yo' ass in the car before I leave you." I wasn't serious, but my tone of voice must have been, because she damn near broke her neck getting to my passenger's door.

As soon as we got into the car and I pulled off, she turned her head around to look out of the back window. "That's the Deacon's block. You don't think we should at least go down there to make sure that everything is okay? What about Purity?"

She raised a good point. Had I come out of the house and saw all them police cars down there, I would have gone straight down there to see if my sister was all good. "Text her for me and ask her if she's okay, and we'll go from there. I don't feel like fucking with all them people right now. You already know how them Houston dicks are. They'll fuck around and snatch me up for nothing, just because they can." Even though I was having her text my sister, I was still getting as far away from our hood as possible. I felt like the longer we stayed in the area, the more she was going to want to go down there and be nosey.

After texting Purity, she sat back in her seat. "Alright, that's done. Now, I'm just gon' see what she say. I'm trying to see if she on Facebook right now, too." She got to playing with her phone while I hit the highway and increased my speed.

I was longing to ser Nikki. I needed to hear her voice, and most of all, just make sure that she was good. We had been through a lot together, and for a few days, I thought that I was going to lose her to the Reaper.

Right before we got to the hospital, I took the back road that comes right before it, that overlooks the river, and pulled my car to the side of the road, while Simone played on her phone. "Look, Simone, chill right here. I gotta piss like a muthafucka."

She waved her hand at me but didn't take her face away from her phone.

I grabbed my book bag out of the back of the car and jogged into the woods about a hundred yards, stomped through some brush, and came upon the river. The sun was just beginning to rise. It was five something in the morning, the day of my birthday, and there I was, down on one knee, pouring alcohol into a towel, drenching it, then cleansing the .45, breaking it down into pieces, before throwing them one at a time over the bridge and into the river. Next, I would do the knife the same way. I saved just enough alcohol to pour onto the book bag, then I set that ablaze, and watched it melt.

After I got back to the car, Simone was texting like crazy. "Holy fuck, Shemar, you not gon' believe this, but the Deacon and his family were killed. At least that's what your sister just texted me. She says she's at the police station, and my mother has to go and get her or they're going to take her to Child Protective Services." Simone looked up to me with eyes full of sorrow. "What are the odds?"

I bucked my eyes and acted like I was at a loss for words.

Luckily, my phone buzzed when it did because I might have given myself away, because I couldn't show no emotion for the Deacon 'nem being killed. Simone grabbed my hand and squeezed it while I read the newest text from our mother, telling me everything that she just said.

Chapter 2

My mother ran into my arms and wrapped them around me, hugging me tight, as soon as I walked through Nikki's hospital room door. She had tears in her eyes. "Baby, they just found Candace, Mark, and the Deacon, dead in their home. It's so sad." She whimpered while I rubbed her back.

"It's gon' be okay, momma, just go and get my sister before they try and take her away again. I don't know what happened, but I can't even fake like I care until I know she's okay. Go get her," I ordered, releasing our hug, and looking her in the eyes while I rubbed her tears away from her cheeks with my thumbs.

She looked me over closely and nodded. "Okay, son. I'll go do that right now. You need to spend some time with Nikki. She's been asking about you a lot. I'll take Simone with me, okay?"

I hugged her again and watched as she grabbed Simone's hand and led her out of the door.

As soon as they disappeared, I looked over to Nikki's bed. She was sitting up, looking at me with her big brown eyes. "Nigga, you can't hug me from there, and that's the least of the things you owe me for taking these slugs fo' yo' ass. Damn. I been missing you like crazy." She smiled, and then shifted her weight uncomfortably in the bed. I could tell that she was still in a lot of pain but acted as if she was trying to brave the elements for me.

As soon as I got to the bed, I leaned my head down and she wrapped her arms around my neck. She smelled like the hospital, but her touch was still soft. I was just thankful that she was alive and able to hug me, period. "I was going crazy, worrying about you, girl. I ain't through sweating niggas either. You know that fool Nut down here too, in honor of you?"

She released her arms from around me, and tried to sit higher in her bed. She was still hooked up to a machine that beeped off and on. She winced in pain before situating herself. "Nigga, I can't tell you was worried about me. When I opened my eyes, you weren't here. Then, I had Mrs. Jones texting you like crazy, but you didn't respond. Damn near broke my heart. You know how much I need you in my corner." She frowned, and crossed her arms in front of her chest.

I shook my head. "N'all it ain't ever like that. I was out there taking care of some business that I'm gon' put you up on in a day or so. Right now, shit kinda hot, so I gotta hold this shit to my chest. On top of that, we had to take a good look at that nigga Mickey over what happened to you, but once again, I ain't gon' get into all that. You know how I get down though, especially about you, so miss me with all that other shit, and just let me hug you right now." I wrapped her into my arms and laid her head on my chest. I missed her so much. I vowed that I would never let her reach harm again.

She hugged me back, then leaned back on her pillow. "You know them people finna sweat the shit out of me as soon as they think I'm well enough to talk. The nurse already told me that they told her that whenever I came out of my coma, to let them know so they could come and find out what happened to me. I hope they ain't trying to do no long ass investigation. You know how much I hate them boys in blue." She adjusted herself on her pillow, and once again winced in pain.

I took my hand and wiped her curly bangs off of her forehead. I wished that she could climb out of that bed and leave the hospital with me, right then. I would go snatch up Purity, and the three of us would just drive until we got as far away from Houston as possible. But it was just wishful thinking. I already knew that them people would have been all over our asses, and then they would have started to connect a few dots too many.

I looked Nikki in her brown eyes. "Nikki, why you ain't tell me that you got into an argument with that nigga Bryan, the day before we robbed his ass? Don't you know that move was stupid as hell, and it's probably the reason why you are laying here right now?"

She avoided my eyes and took a deep breath, before shrugging. "I just never liked that nigga. He always thought he was so hard. Then, he was a straight deadbeat father. I think I would have bodied that nigga, no matter what."

I rubbed her soft cheek with my thumb. "That still don't answer my question. I need to know what made you be so careless, 'cause that nigga knew exactly who you was, and on top of that, Chelsey got a big ass mouth. Well, *had*," I said, alluding to the fact that Chelsey was no longer breathing. I didn't think Nikki knew that, and I wanted to tell her and get that shit over with, because I knew she had a lil' soft spot for her.

Nikki scrunched her face. "Wait, bruh, what you mean had? What you saying to me right now? That she dead or somethin'?" She sat up further on her pillow. This time I noted that she didn't wince in pain. She reached out for me and grabbed my shirt. "Shemar, you smoked my Chelsey? Huh? Keep that shit real with me, homeboy?" I could tell that she was getting angry. Her eyes searched mine deeply. I could tell that she was trying to see inside of my soul.

I looked down at her hand and smiled, then curled my upper lip. She had my collar twisted now, so close to my throat that I could feel her knuckles on my skin. I took a deep breath and tried to calm myself down. "Look, Nikki, I know ole girl was yo' homie and everything, but this shit is bigger than Chelsey. Shawty ran her mouth way too much, so, yeah, she through, but n'all, I ain't kill her. I would have, though."

She tightened her grip on my Polo shirt and clenched her teeth. "Nigga, if you ain't kill her, then who did? Quit playin' with me, Shemar. You know I ain't gon' be in this punk ass bed forever. When I get up out this muhfucka, I'ma touch down to cause hell. Now, you know how I get down."

I mugged her for a long time without saying a word. I couldn't believe that she was acting how she acting over this broad. I felt like my best friend was getting weak and losing herself. I didn't like that shit at all.

"Let my shirt go, and act like you got more love for me than you showing, because right now, you blowin' my mind and I'm feeling some type of way about doing all that I did for you while you was down. Let my fuckin' shirt go, Nikki!" I growled through clenched teeth. I felt myself getting real heated, and I didn't like feeling like that when it was toward her or anybody that I loved. In that moment, I felt like I was ready to put my hands on her, and I had never done that before.

She released me, and kind of pushed me away a lil' bit as she was doing so. "Nigga, you bogus. If you killed that girl, you real bogus, Shemar. You know she the only female that I fuck with on that emotional level. I had a lot of love for her, and she ain't never did shit to cross me." She shook her head while mugging me. "I can't believe you."

I turned my head to the side and just looked her over. I wanted to say do many foul and disrespectful things to her, but I couldn't bring myself to channel that sort of bitch within myself because it just wasn't in me. The bottom line was that I loved Nikki, and that moment just allowed me to see how immature to the game that she really was. I thought that before she had gotten shot that we'd agreed upon her bodying Chelsey anyway, but I guess she had other things in mind.

"You know what, Nikki, you ain't seeing things clear right now because of the blood lost, but I'm just gon' tell you this. By you fuckin around with this broad, and getting involved in her personal life, you just put both of us under the gun with some major niggas in Cloverland. Now I gotta clean up the mess you made, whether you understand that or not. Never the less, I love you, and I'm gon' hold you down until my last breath. You're my heart, and even when you can't see shit clearly, I will for the both of us, because it's my job to protect you at all costs." I turned my back on her and got ready to head for the door.

I couldn't be in that room with her no more. I was getting more and more irritated by the angry look on her face. Besides, I needed to see what was good with Purity and the whole Deacon dilemma. I had to make sure that they stayed off of my trail. I grabbed the handle of the door and turned it, opening it.

"Shemar, wait! Please, wait," Nikki yelled, sitting up in the bed all the way.

I stopped in my tracks and exhaled. "What's good, Nikki? I gotta go check on my sister, man. I ain't finna be standing here, arguing with you all day. This ain't what I came here for."

She nodded. "I know, Shemar, and I'm sorry. I overreacted, but I need you. Please don't leave me in this bed again. Not like this. Not with you feeling how you feeling. I need you." She bit into her bottom lip, before sucking on it.

I shook my head, then slowly walked back over to the bed to sit on the side of it while I wrapped my arm over her shoulder, and allowed for her to lay her head on my chest. "Nikki, I think that bipolar shit acting up with you again. Have these people been giving you yo' medication for that?" I asked, rubbing her shoulder.

She shook her head. "N'all, and you know I don't need that shit. You just caught me off guard with the whole Chelsey thing. That don't mean that I don't love and need you though. I can be mad at you and still need you. Don't forget I am a woman. I should not have to keep telling you that."

24

I leaned down and kissed her on the cheek, holding her more closely, and then there was a knock on the door of her room. I stood straight up and got on point, as a short, dark skinned, pretty, older nurse opened the door and walked into the room, holding a clipboard.

"Hey, Nikki, I see you're awake. That's good." She looked over to me. "And who might this be?" she asked, raising an eyebrow.

Nikki reached out and grabbed my hand. "This is my man. He just flew in from Memphis to check in on me. He goes to the University of Tennessee."

I nodded at her. "How are you doing, ma'am?"

She smiled. "I'm fine, honey, but unfortunately for you, visiting hours are over, and young lady, the detectives are on their way to speak with you. I couldn't stop them from coming, so prepare yourself for a long grilling." She started to check the monitor and write on to her clipboard.

I leaned down and hugged Nikki. "Look, baby, I guess I'll see you later. Get some rest before they get here, and be careful because you already know how they are."

She nodded, and pulled me down to her, wrapping her arms around my neck before kissing me on the lips softly. "I love you, Shemar. If it's one thing I want you to take away from seeing me is that. Don't feel like I ain't just as crazy about you as you are me, because I am. We are all that we have. Loyalty in blood. Forever and always."

As I was leaving her room, I passed two beefy white men dressed in blue suits with badges on their belts. Both of them looked me up and down before turning to the nurse behind the desk that was giving them information about Nikki, I imagined. I say imagined because I couldn't really hear what she was saying to them, but I did note that they were holding a picture of her, along with a clipboard.

As soon as I got into my car, my phone buzzed. It was my mother telling me that she wanted me to meet her at our house as soon as possible.

I pulled up to the house, and the first thing I noted was that there were two police cars parked in front of it. I parked about three houses down and sat behind the wheel for a second. I had to gather myself because I knew that they were going to have to question me a little bit, if not more. I tried to calm myself down and reassure myself that everything was going to be okay.

The sun was out and shining bright, and on the way to the house, I saw plenty kids boarding their school buses, or standing on bus stops. For them, it was a normal day. For me, it was my eighteenth birthday, and I was faced with a whole lot of problems that needed to be sorted out.

I wasn't all the way through the door of the house before Purity ran to me at full speed and jumped into my arms. "Shemar! I missed you so much. The Deacon is dead, and so is Mark and Mrs. Robinson. They think somebody tried to rob the house or something, and Mr. Robinson caught them in the act, and they killed all of them." She hugged me tight while I wrapped my arms around her protectively.

"That's messed up, lil' sis. I'm just glad that you're okay. When did this happen?" I asked, already knowing the answer to that.

A tall, light skinned, detective stood up from the couch, and extended me his hand, before his heavyset, white partner did the same thing. I shook their hands and looked them in the eyes. I was trying to read them as best I could to see if I was a suspect or something.

"Good morning, sir. You must be her brother, Shemar." The light skinned detective said.

I held Purity more firmly to my side. "Yeah, this my sister right here, and I thank y'all for going in there and saving her. She's all I got."

Purity wrapped both of her arms around my waist and looked up at me.

The white detective spoke up. "Well, we didn't have to save her per say. She was able to get out of the house before the shots started going off. Thankfully she left when she did or she would have probably been a basket case like the other three."

The light skinned detective never took his eyes off of me. "Yeah, that would probably be the case. Do you mind if me and you speak in the other room?" he asked, watching me real suspicious like. He looked like an angry version of Sinbad.

I shook my head. "Not at all. Can my sister come along, or should she stay in here with our mother?" I asked, already knowing the answer to that question as well.

He shook his head. "I think it's best if she stays in here with Mrs. Jones. I just have a few questions for you. Nothing major or anything to be alarmed about."

I nodded. "A'ight, that's cool." Looking down at Purity, I said, "Look, sis, stay in here with Mrs. Jones while I holler at this detective. I'll be right back, once I find out what's going on, okay."

She slowly released me. "Okay, but don't be back there forever. I'm scared without you holding me."

Mrs. Jones walked into the living room and handed the detectives a steaming cup of coffee and a Danish. "Aww, it's okay, Purity. I'll hold you until he comes back. Just let him find out what's going on, and then they will be on their way. Okay, baby?"

She nodded. "Yeah, just hurry up, Shemar."

Me and the detectives went down into the den, where they sat on the couch across from me, while I sat on the wicker chair. I already knew they were getting ready to grill me, and I was mentally preparing myself for it.

The light skinned detective sat his coffee and Danish on the glass table that separated us, and pulled out a small notepad. "Can you tell me where you were between the hours of one in the morning and four?"

"Yeah, I was in my room, knocked out and dead to the world. I'd smoked a blunt to the head and I needed to sleep some of my high off." I sat back in the chair, and watched him write some more.

He nodded. "Do you have a prescription for that bud, son?"

I looked at him like he was crazy. "N'all, man."

The white dude laughed. "How was your relationship with your sister's foster parents? You guys have any run-ins? Did you like them? They ever hurt her in any way and it get back to you through her?"

I shrugged. "I didn't really like them or dislike them. I was happy with the fact that they only lived down the street, and that they treated my sister good as far as I knew. Our parents passed away when we were real little, and had they not stepped in, me and my sister would have been split up and probably would have lost contact with each other."

The light skinned detective kept on writing, while the white one continued to grill me. "So, you got this family that's taking care of your sister, treating her nice, and you don't even shed a tear for them being murdered? That's odd."

"My mother always said that you're supposed to cry when a baby is born into this world, not when somebody dies, because they're going to a better place, especially if they believe in Jesus, which the Deacon and his family did. So, there is no need to cry about somebody going to Heaven when we're still stuck right here in this hell we call earth."

The fat white man bit into his Danish and talked with his mouth full. "Now that's deep, kid. That's some real deep shit there."

I shook my head. "If you don't mind, this is a religious home. Please, watch your mouth and refrain from using that vulgar language."

He smiled. "Ouch. Excuse me." He took a sip of his coffee. "Do you know anyone that could have done this to their family? I mean, this is pretty gruesome stuff. We haven't seen murders like this for a long time. Somebody hated these people, and you're just lucky that your sister wasn't present or she could have very well been a goner. Had that happened, do you think you would have cried? "

I nodded. "Yeah. But I would have cried for my own selfish reasons, and not for the ones you would have thought I was crying for." I knew they were trying to trip me up by playing with my head, so I decided to dance with them a little bit and give them what they were asking for.

The light skinned detective stopped writing on his pad and looked up at me. "What do you mean by that? Enlighten me."

I scooted forward in the seat and clasped my fingers together. "I would have cried because I could no longer see and be with my sister, physically, every single day. I would miss her, and always wonder what she was doing from time to time. But at the same time, there would have been tears of joy because I would have known that she was with our Father in Heaven, and that would be a blessing."

They looked at me for a long time, and then looked at each other. I couldn't really tell what they were thinking, but I was going to continue my charade as long as they kept messing with me. Finally, they stood up at almost the same time.

"Well, you have a whole house of women that need your consoling. If I were you, I would keep a close eye on Purity. She may have some intense nightmares for a while. She's going to need your protection," said the white one.

The light skinned one handed me his card. "If you come across any new information that could be helpful to this investigation, I would urge you to give me a call. Can you promise me you'll do that?" he asked, picking up his cup of coffee and taking a sip from it. "Umm, pretty good." He continued to look at me over the rim of his cup.

I wasn't into make promises to nobody if I didn't intend on keeping them, and just because dude was the police, didn't mean that I was gon' step outside of my values as a man. "I really don't know nothin', so you can't really depend on me. But you gentlemen have a good day." I walked them upstairs and my mother took over from there.

Ghost

Chapter 3

I wound up chilling in the crib for the next three weeks with Purity all under me. I mean, she barely ever left my sight. It didn't even dawn on me that I missed celebrating my own birthday until Simone's was one day away. She was three weeks and a year younger than me, and her birthday party was all that she could talk about, alongside the Robinson family murders. Due to the fact that nobody from their family was able to stand in for Purity, Mrs. Jones was granted temporary custody, pending a hearing before a family court judge, but that was scheduled to be months down the line.

Nut hit me up the night before Simone's birthday on business. He was Nikki's cousin and had come to Houston to surprise her. Once he found out that she'd been shot up, he lost it and got on that gangsta shit with me, bodying niggas in search of who'd put that led to his cousin. The homie was from Brooklyn, and he was definitely about that life.

"Yo, Sun, I need to touch bases with you in regards to that one move that lil' homie was barking about. Meet me at my room, ASAP," he said through his deep voice.

I hung up the phone and met him an hour later after damn near begging Purity to unwrap her arms from around me. She ain't wanna let me out of her sight or out of the house, and every time I tried to leave the crib, she would break down crying, saying that she was worried about me. Even though it pulled on my heart strings, after three weeks, I needed some fresh air. Plus, me and Nut had some unfinished business that had to be tended too.

Before all of that shit went down with the Deacon and his family, me and him had been on business, trying to find out who had shot Nikki's crib up. In the midst of fucking a few niggas over, some cat named Mickey had caught a few slugs from our pistols, but was still able to get away before we could finish his ass, so there was still some work that had to be done, especially since he was working under a major power player by the name of Sherm. He'd be the next hit on our list.

As soon as I stepped into the room, Nut gave me a half of hug and palmed the back of my head. I guessed this was a custom they did out there in New York, but I didn't like it. I didn't like nobody gripping my shit like that.

"Yo, what's good, Sun? Long time no see. Word is bond. I been gettin' antsy as hell, waiting on yo' ass to get back in tune with me. How is Nikki?" he asked, releasing the back of my head.

I ran my hand over my three sixty waves, trying to fix what I assumed he had messed up in the pattern. "Say, big homie, I don't like all that east coast shit you be doing to my head, man. Y'all too touchy-feely and shit." I mugged him just a lil' bit, irritated while closing the door behind me, and locking it. "Nikki good. She finally out of that coma. I ain't been able to jam with you because I had some other shit I had to tend to in regards to my sister, and you already know I don't fuck with them phones like that, playboy. Them bitches is indictments waiting to happen, which is why I ain't fill you in like I wanted to.

Anyway, what's good?" I walked over and sat on the bed, while he grabbed a blunt out of the ashtray and lit the tip.

"That nigga, Tim say, he got some shit set up for us to holler at Sherm punk ass tonight. He having a lil' family get together, and the lil' homie supposed to be on security, along with a few other niggas. He gon' let us storm the door he guarding so we can body this nigga and wipe him off the list. That fool Mickey done bounced back too. He caught three to the back, and all them bitches missed his spine. I don't know when he supposed to be getting out of the hospital, but the streets saying he on a shit bag now, so you know Sun gon' want his revenge. So far, he ain't went to the law, but ain't no telling how long that's gon' last." Nut took a strong pull off of the blunt with his jaws puffed out, inhaled, and took two more pulls before passing the Loud to me.

I took it and took three strong pulls. Right away I felt the smoke carve at my inner chest, took two more pulls, inhaled them, then passed him the blunt back. "Bruh, if we fucking with lil' Tim, and we gon' honor his word, then I'm with it. I say we holla at that nigga Sherm tonight and get this shit over with. The last thing I wanna be doing is looking over my shoulder every second. That nigga Mickey definitely know who I am, and he know why we were getting at him because we told him. I let his baby momma go too, but so far I ain't seen her on the news or on Facebook saying shit about what happened that night. I think she honored how I handled shit with her and her kid. At least, I hope so."

Nut waved me off. "Fuck that, Kid. I see that bitch, I'm bodying her too. That's how this game go. You can't be selective about who you hit because the muhfuckas that you let go'll be the same muhfuckas that take that stand on you later on, so I ain't going. The only way I'ma be able to sleep at night is if I know everybody that got anything to do with this situation is dead, that includes lil' dawg when it's all said and done. Word is bond."

That caught me off guard. I didn't know he was thinking about stanking our lil' homie. That made me start to think that I was on his list as well. I had to play this nigga real close because I really didn't know him like that. All I knew about him was that he was Nikki's cousin and she had always told me that he was an animal out there in Brooklyn. I didn't know entirely what that meant, but I was definitely gon' have her put me up on this nigga, or I saw myself killing him first. I rarely trusted niggas to begin with. I was just about to ask him why he was considering stanking Tim, when there was a knock on the door.

I pulled my .9 out of the small of my back, and stepped into the bathroom, closing the door a lil' bit, but kept it open enough for me to put the barrel of my gun out of it. I had plans on bucking whoever it was at the door if they were an enemy, even though I knew that enemies rarely knocked.

Nut frowned and picked up the .40 Glock off of the nightstand. Then, he held up one hand to me, before putting his ear on the door. "Man, who is it?" he asked, cocking back the Glock.

I couldn't hear what the answer was, but I was ready to buss. I saw Nut's whole demeanor change to that of relief. He slowly opened the door and stood back.

Tim walked in, in an all Gucci outfit, with the up-side-down sun visor on his head. He had his cell-phone to his ear and a blunt in his other hand. He was still talking on the phone when Nut closed the door behind him. A few minutes later, he hung up and they gave each other half hugs. Nut gripped the back of his head, and when they parted I noted that Tim ran his hand over his waves just like I did. I silently laughed at that, and came out of the bathroom with my pistol at my hip.

As soon as he saw me, his eyes got big as saucers. "Shemar, nigga, I'm surprised you still alive. That nigga Sherm got the whole Cloverland gunning for you. Now that nigga done put the bounty on yo' head up to fifty racks, and that's dead or alive. Mickey been running his mouth like Wendy Williams. It's a few niggas got shot that they thought was you. The pressure is on." He walked over to me and I gave him a half hug as well, though I ain't grip the back of his head or no shit like that. I was from Houston, not Brooklyn.

After we broke our embrace. I nodded. "So, what's good with this move tonight? You sure eve-rything gon' be on the up and up? This nigga gon' be here, and the door you guarding, we gon' be able to get through that muhfucka with no problem?"

Tim sat on the bed and pulled out a pill bottle. He took out two of the pills and got to crushing them on the table with a pumice stone. After they were crushed to dust, he made four lines and snorted up the first one. He wiped his nose, then leaned his head down and tooted up another one using his right nostril instead of his left, like the first line. After that, he wiped his nose again, and popped a pieces of candy into his mouth. I was looking at this nigga like he was crazy, and so was Nut. I had never known the lil' homie to toot shit.

He nodded. "Yeah, everything gon' go smooth. That nigga Sherm don't think I got enough balls to cross him. Most cats wouldn't, but I'm trying to eat with you niggas. I got a whole lot of hungry niggas that need to nibble off of my plate. I'm tryna feed all of them and take over Cloverland with you, Shemar. We been here since the womb, and it's time we get a piece of the pie. We knock off this nigga Sherm and its a corner of the Dope Land that's gon' be wide open for us to take over. I know you got them plugs. I got the niggas. We can bully our way into this shit and really eat. Fuck Sherm, man. Let's hit that nigga." He leaned his head down and got to tooting his pills again.

Nut kept smoking his blunt, and my mind was doing a lil' racing. Even though I had a lil' love for Tim, I didn't know how much I could trust him. But if it was true that Sherm was steady upping the price tag on my head, and that Mickey was running his mouth, then I really ain't have no choice but to take this bone that Tim was throwing to me, because there was no telling when my clock would run out. Fifty gees was a lot of money for any nigga in the hood. I would have personally bodied two niggas for that amount of paper, just as long as I was paid twenty-five bands up front. I just had to do what I had to, and play both Tim and Nut close to my chest. I didn't trust neither one of them, and I already knew I was gon' wind up taking both of them out of the game one day, but I would pick my moment. Strategy was everything.

Nut walked over to Tim and laid his big hand on his shoulder. "Sun, what's that shit you putting up yo' nose?" He blew his weed smoke to the ceiling.

Tim's eyes were low now. He looked like he was zoning. "Aw, man, that's dem Oxys. These muhfuckas take all my pain away. Ever since my car accident, I been fucked up. With them, I'm good."

Nut shook his head. "I guess, Kid. Just keep a handle on that shit. You driving down a slippery road."

My mind was still racing like crazy. "Say, Tim, what time is the best time to make all of this shit happen?" I wanted to get at Sherm's chin. The more I thought about him putting cash on my head, the more irritated I became until I was seeing red.

He pulled out his phone and got to reading something on it that I couldn't see. Then, he sat on the bed and nodded. "Money Bag Yo coming to town tonight, and Sherm having his after-party directly afterwards. That's when its best to hit his ass. Y'all should wait until about three in the morning, then come and turn that bitch out. I'll be on point. I still get my chips, right?"

I nodded. "Most definitely."

Afterward, we would sit back and get a complete understanding as to how we was finna hit this nigga. Me and Nut decided that we would link back up at about two, so I decided that I would roll back to the crib to try and clear my head. Besides all of that, Purity had hit my phone over twenty times, asking me where I was and saying that she missed me, and that she was scared being there without me. I felt a lil' bad for her, because back, then I didn't really understand how me killing three people that she had grown up with since she was eight years old really affected her mentally. I didn't have the mental maturity to think that far, back then. I just thought I did my part by protecting her and getting them out of the way, but it went way deeper than that for a female.

When I got back to the house, I made it through the crib and saw that she was asleep on the couch with a blanket wrapped over her. I imagined that she had been up waiting for me, and finally her body gave out from exhaustion. The last few weeks following the murders, she hadn't slept more than two hours a day, so I think it was catching up with her. I leaned down and kissed her on the forehead. I was about to wake her up when I felt two hands slide over my shoulders. I turned around so fast that I almost fell onto Purity.

My mother smiled, and put a finger up to her lips. "Be quiet, and come here, baby," she whispered, taking my hand and leading me to the back of the house where her room was located.

On the way, Simone opened her bedroom door, saw that I was home, stepped into the hallway, and grabbed my arm. "Shemar, come here. I need to talk to you for a minute." She sounded needy and like she was about to cry. She kept on looking over my shoulder at our mother as if she was worried or something.

I frowned after reading her body language. "What's the matter, Simone? Why you look like you about to cry and stuff?" I walked up on her, but my mother pulled me closer to her own body.

"Look, I'll send him in there to talk to you once we finish in here. Right now, I need to talk to him, and its important, so you go in there and finish your homework like I told you before, or there will be no birthday party tomorrow. Do you understand me, Simone?" She asked more sternly than I had ever heard her before.

Simone lowered her head and dropped my arm. "Yes. Shemar, when y'all done talking, can you please come and holler at me? It's important." She looked up at me with glossy eyes. It made me want to console her right away.

I nodded. "Yeah, I'll be in there. Just chill for a minute and do like momma say. You good." I leaned forward and kissed her on the cheek.

She smiled, placed her hand over where I'd kissed her, and slowly walked into her room. "Don't forget, big bruh."

I shook my head. "I won't."

As soon as my mother got me into her room, she closed the door behind us, then came up to me and pushed me backward until my back was against the wall. Then, she stood on her tippy toes and kissed my lips. She turned her head to the side, sucked them, licked them, trailed her hands under my shirt, rubbing all over my chest while she kissed me some more, moaning into my mouth with her eyes closed.

She was a little thicker than Simone, and all woman, and no matter what she did she always found a way to turn me on like crazy, and had been ever since she adopted me. I had to grip that big ass booty, while I snaked my tongue into her mouth and sucked all over her thick lips. They were juicy and tasted like cherry for some reason.

"Umm. Baby, I been feening for you for damn near a month. I need some of you tonight, and I ain't taking no for an answer. Ain't I been doing everything that you tell me to do?" She moaned, unbuckling my Ferragamo belt, and then unbuttoning my Robin jeans, before her hands snaked their way into my boxers, gripping my dick real tight.

I squeezed her booty, and ran my hand under her globes, pulling her gown up along the way. Underneath she was naked. Her pussy felt hot and a little damp already. I ran my fingers over her sex lips, pinching them slightly before sliding my middle finger deep into her center, causing her to stand on her tippy toes more.

She moaned and pulled my pants and boxers all the way down. Afterward, she dropped to her knees, grabbing my dick and stroking it, before kissing the head and licking it. "Son, I want you in me right now. We gotta hurry up while yo' sister sleep. I just wanna bend over this bed while you hit me from the back, real hard like I love. Momma need her baby worse than ever. You understand me?" she asked, sucking me into her mouth with her hand moving back and forth while she stroked my dick.

I closed my eyes for a minute, just enjoying how good everything was feeling. Her mouth was packed with heat, and the harder she sucked me the closer I was to cumming. It didn't take me long to get super hard. As soon as I did, she stood up and bent over the bed, and pulled her gown up, spreading her feet apart and looking at me over her shoulder.

"Come on, baby. Hurry up. I need you," she whimpered.

By this time, I was so hard that my dick was sticking all the way out in front of me like a dark brown flashlight or something. I wanted that pussy bad. I mean, even though I was a foot away from entering her, I was feening for it. I walked up to her, took my head and put it on her sex lips, and eased my way into her furnace. It made me shiver. He walls sucked at me, and her pussy was so wet that it was leaking down her thighs, just like her daughter's. I grabbed her hips and stabbed forward, hard, pulled all the way back and stabbed forward again, before I got to killing that shit.

"Un-a! Un-a! Yes, baby. Yes, son. Fuck me. Unn-a. Unn-a. Just like that. Unn-a. Just like. Just like. Unn-a. Just like that. Unn-a. Unn-a. Uhhh. Yes!" She bounced back into me, looking over her shoulder at me. I think she liked to watch me fuck her. She was obsessed with me being her son, and I felt like it was just for these purposes, because every time I got on that ass, she was super wet and it never took her that long to cum.

I used to think that it was because of her that my dick was so big, because shortly after she adopted me, she started pulling on him a lot. Now I know I'm supposed to feel some type of way about that for the negative, but I just can't. I loved her pussy, and all that forbidden shit that came along with it. I grabbed her hair, and made her arch her back while I wore that ass out. She bounced back into my lap, and I was breathing heavy as hell, absorbing her heat, and the scent that came up from between her legs.

"Fuck me, baby. Fuck, mommy. Yes. Unnnn-a. I'm cumming, baby. Momma. Cummiinngg. Uhhhh-yes babbeee-a." She started to slam back into me so hard that I had to grab her hips, and bend my knees a lil' bit.

Her and Simone acted just alike every time I fucked them from then from the back. Just imagining me having both of them bent over the bed caused me to cum.

I clenched my teeth and threw my head back. Slamming into her with sexual anger, again and again, until I couldn't take it no more. I reached under her and grabbed a hold of them titties. Her nipples were poking me in the palms of my hands. Then, I came deep within her box, growling like a fucking Pitbull, ready to strike. As soon as she felt it, she started to work her pussy muscles as only an older woman could. Milking me and whipping me in the process. It wasn't nothing like that vet pussy. I still stand by that to this day.

Chapter 4

It was about 2:30 in the morning, and there I was on the other side of town. I slid a .9 millimeter into the small of my back, put a .45 on my hip, and a .380 in my right pocket, before I slid my white ski mask down my head.

Nut sat in the driver's seat with a Tech .9 on his lap, and he'd already loaded up his hand guns. He looked angry. "Yo, Kid, I'm telling you now, I'm hitting everything in sight. We ain't got time to be playin' with these niggas, man. If Sun will put up fifty bands on ya' head, then that mean that he fear you, Kid. The worst enemy to have is the one that fear you. Word is bond."

He pulled a small blank envelope out of his pocket, opened it and stuck his pinky nail into it, pulling up some white powder. He snorted it into his left nostril, then he did the same thing with the right one. This blew my mind because I didn't even know he got down like that.

I scrunched my face and tucked the bottom of my mask into my shirt's collar just in case somebody tried to pull it out in the midst of a struggle to reveal my identity. Though it had never happened before, I still wanted to be careful and fully on point. "Nigga, what's that, right there?" I asked, pointing to the envelope that he was tooting out of again.

He put his pinky nail full of the powder back to his left nostril and snorted it up, hard. "Yo, this them Purk thirties, Kid. I like to get hyped up on this shit. Just in case I eat a few slugs, I won't feel shit. I fuck with them Oxys too, but I ain't ran across them joints since I been back in town, and I ain't tryna fuck with Tim and put him in my business. So, the next best thing is Percocet's. You wanna try this shit?" He put the envelope by my face, and I pushed his hand away without too much force.

I ain't wanna spill the contents or nothin'. "Bruh, I'm good. I can't develop no habits right now. I got way too much shit on my plate fa that."

He shrugged. "Nigga, suit yo' self. You might not be fuckin' with it right now, but in time, you will. Pills is the new weed, even back out East, Kid." He grabbed up a pinky full and tooted it up his right nostril. "Awww! Sss!" He clenched his teeth together. "Now I'm ready to wet some shit, Sun. Word is bond."

I shook my head, and opened the passenger's door. "Let's go, nigga. Let's get this shit over with." We had parked a few blocks away and had decided to take the alleys all the way to Sherm's crib.

Majority of the lights were shot out that were supposed to light up the alley, and to be honest, I felt like that pushed things into our favor because the less people that were able to identify us, the better. The way Nut was talking, he had plans on wetting everything in sight if it came down to that. So, that meant that it was going to be mass hysteria. The more people, the more chances it gave us of being captured by camera phone, or somebody's eyes, period. The odds would have been crazy. Due to the fact that the lights on our escape route were out, I was just thankful for that.

It felt like it was every bit of eighty degrees out, and a lil' humid this night. As soon as we were about a block away from the after party, I started to see all kinds of foreign cars rollin' around, bumping different songs from Money Bag Yo. Looking from the alley and down a few gangways, I could see females walking down the block, headed in the direction of Sherm's house; I imagined ready to get their party on, not knowing that the Angels of Death were going to be crashing the party real soon. Tim said that he was in charge of guarding the backdoor to the house, and that was the door we intended on going through.

When we got to the back of the house, there was a male and a female just going into the house. I saw that, as the woman walked inside of the house with her hand being held by her man, Tim looked down and checked out her ass, put his fist to his mouth, and shook his head. She was dressed in a real short Gucci dress that showed off the bottoms of her ass cheeks and thick thighs. Even from where I was perched, I could see that she was strapped.

Nut straightened his white ski mask and cocked back his Tech. "Let's go holler at these niggas, Kid, and remember what I told you. I'm letting muhfuckas have it. So, you better too." He jumped up and ran across the yard toward the back door.

As soon as he took off, I ran right behind him. My heart was throbbing in my chest. I didn't know how many people I was about to kill. I was hoping it would only be Sherm and a few of his niggas, but there was no tellin'. I was just gon' go with the flow.

We made it to the back door, I knocked once, and I heard Tim's voice on the other side. "Who is it, and what's the password?"

I frowned. Password? What the fuck was this nigga talkin' 'bout? We had never discussed nothin' about a password. "Password is it's us, nigga, open the doe."

It seemed like he nearly broke his neck trying to get it open, and just as I was about to bum rush the spot, he stepped out of the house looking over his shoulder. "Aye. Look, y'all ain't gotta do shit like that. You niggas can just go inside and blend in. That fool Sherm about to be shutting this bitch down in less than an hour, so they can have an after-after party with the hoes. If y'all chill, y'all won't have to body so many people, because only a chosen few gon' stay back. Trust me." He looked a lil' worried and I was wondering if it had anything to do with him having second thoughts about everything.

Nut shook his head. "N'all. Fuck that, Kid. That's too much work. We finna run through this bitch and handle business, just like we discussed. How many niggas on security in here?" he asked, slightly bumpin' Tim out of the way.

Tim swallowed, and once again looked over his shoulders at the door. "It's like five hitters in there with hand guns, but they drunk ass fuck though. They roaming around the party, Sherm is upstairs fucking with this Asian and Black stripper bitch, getting a private dance. If you gon' fuck him over, now is the best time, because he fucked up off of that Raw." Tim shook his head. "Fuck, if y'all gon' do this shit then let's go." He reached into his drawers and pulled out a black ski mask, threw it over his head and pulled it down.

Behind us, I could hear the song "She Doin' It" by Money Bag Yo come onto the speakers throughout the house. Tim pulled a .44 off of his hip and cocked it back, before opening the door and running into the house. He wasn't in for more than a second when I heard his gun go off. *Boom!* Then, he jumped back into me. I looked over his shoulder and saw a big, fat dark skinned nigga laying on his back with a hole in his forehead. Blood slowly poured out of it and dripped down his face.

"Bitch ass nigga. I never liked you anyway. Let's go, big homie." I shook the cob webs from my brain and stepped over the fat nigga, running up the stairs where there was a closed door. The music was so loud that I could barely hear myself think.

I thought that Tim was about to open this door, but he shook his head. "N'all, bruh, that fool upstairs. Let's kill his ass and take over his set in Cloverland. You already know how this shit go." He started to climb the stairs with me, and Nut behind him.

My heart was still racing. I didn't know what I was walking into, but I wanted to get it over and done with. Tim had killed a nigga right in front of us, and I didn't even know that he had that shit in him. My mind was slightly blown.

When we got upstairs, there was another locked door. Tim went into his pants and came up with a key, putting it into the lock, before opening it. I couldn't believe that they had trusted him so much that he had all of the access that he did. I filed that away in my memory to never put more trust in him than I had to, because obviously he had a way about gaining trust from people before he used it to benefit himself. I honored his intelligence and I would never under estimate the lil' nigga.

He pushed in the door, and it opened up to a short hallway, which I ran right into with him and Nut behind me. At the front of the hallway was the living room, and I could see that there was a dude in there with a thick ass red bone on his lap. She had her back to his chest, giving him a sensual lap dance while the music blared out of the speakers. The entire upstairs smelled like plenty weed smoke.

I ran full speed in the direction of the living room, while Nut stopped short in the hallway and kicked in a door, and then his guns got to going off back to back. It sounded like constant thunder. This made the red bone that was sitting on dude's lap jump up, and as soon as she did, he reached on the side of him and came up with a sawed-off Gauge. He aimed it in my direction and bussed. *Boom!* The bullet whipped past my face and slammed into the fish tank that was to my left. I lit his ass up, giving him all chest and face shots. *Boom! Boom! Boom! Boom!*

He fell back into the couch while the holes filled him up and ate away his flesh. I held my smoking gun while I looked him over. He didn't look familiar, but I didn't care. I figured if he was in the house with Sherm, then he had to have some type of connections to him.

The red bone started screaming at the top of her lungs until I grabbed her by the throat and slung her to floor. "Shawty, shut yo' ass up before I have to kill you. You wanna die like this nigga right here? Huh?" I asked.

She shook her head. "No! Please. I was just having some fun."

"Shut up, and lay yo' ass behind this couch, because if my niggas see you, they gon' body you, and I ain't gon' be able to save you. Hurry up!" I hollered, looking down the hallway, expecting to see either Nut or Tim.

She stepped over the man's dead body, and jumped over the back of the couch. I could still hear her whimpering like crazy.

"Shut up, shawty. I don't wanna kill you because you ain't got shit to do with this."
As I was scolding her, I could hear what sounded like chaos downstairs. I was guessing that people heard the shots up here and were making a run for it. I know that's what I would have done.

I heard more gun shots, then Tim ran out of one of the rooms with his gun smoking. "Deez niggas dead, and them two hoes. It's a new day, my nigga." He ran into the room right next to this, and I followed him inside. What I saw caught me completely off guard.

Nut had his Tech down the nigga Sherm's throat, and a .45 down the throat of the Asian and Black stripper. When we came through the door, he looked over his shoulder. "Shemar, this that bitch ass nigga Sherm, right here. I was gon' blow his brains out, but seeing as you here, I'm gon' leave that shit up to you."

Boom! Boom! The stripper's head jerked backward twice, and then her brains splattered across the headboard. It was blood all over it. Nut stood up but kept the barrel down Sherm's throat.

"But that bitch had to go, though."

She slowly slid down the headboard before falling off of the bed, onto her bloody face. It was then that I could see the massive hole in the back of her head, and the brain matter that sailed down her neck. I shook my head.

Tim stepped forward and pulled his mask up, extending his gun, putting it to Sherm's forehead. "Bitch ass nigga, you thought I was scared of yo' punk ass, but it's a new day. I grind fo' the homie Shemar now. We take yo' key to the streets." He moved out of the way. "Finish this nigga, Shemar, and let's get the fuck up out of here."

I stepped forward with my upper lip curled, imagining how Nikki looked when she first got shot up and was fighting for her life. There were a few things that I wanted to say to him, but I decided against it.

So, as Nut pulled his barrel out of Sherm's mouth, he looked like he wanted to jump up and run. "Man, please. Y'all can have whatever y'all want. Don't kill me. I got two hundred and—"

Boom! Boom! Boom! Boom! Boom! Boom! His body leaped from the bed, again and again, as each bullet tore into his flesh. I kept on fingering fucking my .45, imagining Nikki. My loyalty was everything to me.

After my gun started to click, we got the fuck up out of there. Time was of the essence. As we got down the stairs, we were met by a group of females with barely any clothes on. As soon as they saw our masks, they started screaming at the top of their lungs, and tried to run in the opposite direction, falling all over each other. It was chaotic.

Two security guards for Sherm came out of the downstairs apartment and upped their guns, aiming in our direction, and started bussing. *Boom! Boom! Boom! Boom!* Those were the sounds of the shots ringing again and again.

I ducked down, then shot out of the back door toward the yard. Nut turned around and let his Tech spit rapidly. *Pop-pop-pop! Pop-pop-pop! Pop-pop-pop!* Then, Tim was dumping at them. *Boom! Boom! Boom!* I hit a fence, ran through that backyard and wound up in the alley, running full speed past a group of females that were running as fast as they could, I guessed.

More shots rang out behind me, but I was too busy trying to get away to see what was going on. I figured that Nut and Tim had it all taken care of, and I was right.

Sherm had all of that power in Cloverland, but in my opinion, it had been almost too easy to smoke that nigga. I made a vow to myself to never get caught slipping like he did, or ever grow too relaxed in the game. I would trust no man like the homie Cash taught us in his books. The game was not to be taken lightly, but as deadly as it was, I wanted my piece of the Slums. That shit was in me.

Chapter 5

A week later, Simone woke me up and blew my mind. It had to be about 2AM, and I had decided to lay low in the crib for a whole week because Cloverland was super-hot and flooded with police after the Sherm's After Party Murders, which was just what they were calling it. I mean, there were patrol cars rolling up and down the streets, only minutes after one another. There were also detectives knocking on doors, asking questions about that night. It was all the kids talked about at school and on Facebook. I was tired of hearing about it.

We had attended the Robinson family funerals only two days prior, and I was still trying to mentally get right with God because I was feeling sick in the head. There I was, the one that had murdered them, at their funerals acting like I was grieving with their surviving family, along with my own. I felt like the devil himself. The funeral was also filled with cops.

Simone woke me up by pushing me in the chest slightly. I was laying on my back with Purity's head on one side of my chest, and the other side was bare. I remember it being a lil' hot this day in the house. "Shemar. Shemar. Boy, will you wake up already?" She smacked me on the chest, and that made me open my eyes, and sit up part way.

Purity's head fell off of me and onto the pillow. "Oww." She opened her eyes. "What's going on?" I could tell that she was still sleepy and super irritated.

Simone put her finger to her lips. "Shhh. I gotta talk to Shemar. It's real important. You go back to sleep." She made a face that said she was a little annoyed as well. Purity and Simone never really got along, and deep down I think it was because of me.

I felt like both of them wanted me all the time, and I could only spread myself out so far. I mean, it really didn't bother me with how needy they were, and I was glad that I was the one that they needed instead of some other off-brand nigga that wasn't worthy of them in any way. At least I knew I would die for either one of them with no hesitation.

I pulled the covers back and sat on the edge of the bed, trying to gain my senses. "You sure this can't wait until the morning?" I asked Simone before yawning.

Purity wrapped her arm around my waist and laid her head on my thigh. "Yeah, we were sleeping real good until you ruined it."

Simone scrunched her face, then rolled her eyes. "Damn, Purity, he my brother, too. Can I spend some time with him some time?"

Purity yawned and covered her mouth before laying her open hand on my abs and slowly rubbed them. "I don't care, just as long as you ain't waking us up all the time."

I watched Simone mug the shit out of Purity's hand, then she curled her upper lip and grabbed my arm, pulling me from the bed. "Let's go to my room, Shemar. What I got to tell you is a secret, and for your ears only; not for little kids." She mugged Purity.

I stretched and stood up in my boxers, fitting my feet into my house slippers and following Simone out of the room.

"Don't be in there all day, Shemar, you know I can't sleep without you." Purity whimpered.

As soon as the door closed, Simone went on a verbal rampage while I sat on her bed, and smacked my lips. I hoped I didn't have to talk much because my breath tasted funny. "What's good, Simone?"

She locked her bedroom door and started to pace the floor, shaking her head like she was about to blow up. "Look, Shemar, I know that's yo' sister and all, but fuck that. She got me jealous as hell. I hate even thinking about how she laid up in the bed with you, rubbing all over my fucking abs. Don't you know what that does to a girl? Sister or not?"

I ran both of my hands over my face and was starting to get irritated because I was hoping that she didn't call me in the room for that, that early in the morning. "Simone, I know this ain't what you called me in here for, right?" I looked up at her with my eye brow raised.

She shook her head. "N'all, but I just hate that shit. I wanna lay in the bed with you at night. I want you to hold me, and put yo' dick all on my ass while we spooning. Why should she be the only one in this house getting that treatment when we all want you in that way, including her, probably." She continued to pace while I held my head down.

I was sleepy as hell, and I didn't feel like arguing with her, especially about Purity. My sister loved to be all under me. I didn't see nothing wrong with that. She had been through a lot, and for a long time we were forced to live in different households. Now that we were under the same roof, she just wanted to be with me as much as possible. "Simone, what did you call me in here for? You better tell me quick or I'm finna go back to sleep and holler at you in the morning." I yawned again, covering my mouth.

She turned around and faced me. "You gon' sleep in here with me? I need you to hold me. I'm feeling sick right about now." She dropped down to her knees in front of me. "Please, Shemar." She leaned her head back into my collar bone. "Can you just spend the rest of the night with me and give me some lovey-dovey time?" She laid her head on my knee and wrapped her arms around my calve muscle. "You don't understand what I'm going through emotionally. This shit is not a game."

I took a deep breath and exhaled. She was right. I honestly didn't know what she was going through emotionally, and due to the fact that it was the middle of the night and I was sleepy as hell, I really didn't have the mental capacity to try and figure it out. I was getting more aggravated then anything.

I unwrapped her arms and pulled her up so she was standing right in front of me. Looking into her pretty face, noting how bad she looked, even with her hair wrapped up in a blue scarf. I couldn't do nothing but smile, even though I was annoyed as hell. I rubbed the sides of her face with my thumbs while I looked into her brown eyes. "Simone, tell me why you woke me up tonight. What is on your mind? I'm here to listen." I pulled her so that she was sitting on my lap. I wrapped my right arms around her waist and put my chin on her shoulder, sniffing her up a lil' bit. Her Prada perfume went up my nose and intoxicated me like it always did. I loved how she felt in my arms. Always had.

She exhaled. "Shemar, I don't want you to be mad because I didn't do nothin' on purpose, even though I know you finna think that. But I just need you to look at things from my point of view and understand that it's killing me. Okay?" She turned around to look into my face so she could see my response.

By this time, that morning wood was getting the better of me. I situated her so that she was sitting directly onto the center of my lap. That soft ass felt awesome. Once her cheeks trapped my piece, I was good to listen. I was familiar with her overreacting to damn near everything, so I didn't think whatever she had to say was going to be a really huge deal. I just felt like her emotions were getting the better of her, and I was gon' try and do everything that I could to ease her heart, because I truly cared about her.

I nodded. "Awright, I'm gon' hear you out and take how whatever you about to tell me into consideration of how it affects you first, and then myself. I got you, baby. You know that." I kissed her behind the ear, and sucked on her neck. It was hot and tasted good to my tongue.

She nodded. "Okay, I believe you, but still, let me turn around so I can face you while I tell you what I have to. Hold on." She turned all the way around and put one thigh over each one of my own until we were basically forehead to forehead.

I could smell her all the more, and in my mind, there was nothing like the scent of a woman. Her arms wrapped around my neck, and we looked into each other's eyes. Her browns peering into my hazel ones.

I reached around and gripped that big ass, holding it in my hands. "Okay, now tell me what's on your mind." I leaned forward and kissed her soft lips, sucking on the bottom one real quick; loving her taste.

She took both of her hands and held my face. "Shemar, I love you. I have always loved you, and I always will. You the only brother that I have ever known, and you are my first and only unconditional love that I will do anything for. I absolutely hate sharing you, and I wish I could have you all to myself. I would do anything to make this happen." She took a deep breath and slow exhaled, loudly. "Now, with that being said, just know that I would never try and trap you, but things happen for a reason, and we can't control them." She took another deep breath.

Now, I was starting to get a little nervous. I was trying to think of anything that she could possibly say that would make her have to set it up like she had. I started thinking about the Robinson family murders, and wondered if she was finna tell me that she had given the detectives some information in regards to that night, and now she was feeling guilty about it and wanted to get it off of her chest. My head was spinning, and I just needed to know what she was about to say already. "Simone, what's good? Holla at me."

She held my face more firmly in her hands, and searched my eyes real closely. "Shemar, I'm pregnant with our child. You and I are going to be parents, and I need to know what you want to do, because whatever you say, I'll do. I just don't want to lose you. Ever." She looked me over for another second, then laid her head on my chest. "Please, don't be mad, baby. Please."

My heart started beating so fast that I thought it was going to explode. All I could do was hold her. I had a baby on the way already? Really? At the age of eighteen? And by Simone? Aw shit, this was going to mess some things up. First, I didn't know how we were going to tell our mother. Second, I didn't know what her father would say. Third, that was a responsibility that was going to eat me alive, because I knew that I would go hard for my child, and always keep it first and foremost in life. Simone would never have to worry about anything again. I would make sure that I went above and beyond to keep her straight. I was never a sucka. This news just meant that I was gon' have to man up and get my chips all the way up even more now.

Simone hugged me tighter. "Baby, please say something. I am begging you. You gon' make me have a heart attack if you don't." Just then, there was a knocking at her bedroom door. She jumped off of my lap and put her ear to it. Her gown had gotten stuck on the small of her back, revealing her fluffy brown ass cheeks. Panties were nowhere in sight. "Who is it?" She whispered, and I could tell that she was a little choked up.

"It's Purity. Can you tell Shemar that I need to talk to him?"

Simone rolled her eyes and put her hand on her hip, looking at the door while shaking her head.

I sat on the edge of the bed with my head down.

"Look, Purity, he'll be in there in a minute. We're talking about something very important right now,"

Simone said with a mug on her face. She started to shake her head all over again.

Purity beat on the door a little harder. "I don't care what you guys are doing! I want to say something to my brother! Now open this door before I start kicking on it!" She threatened. It sounded like she was getting ready to cry.

I jumped off of the bed and moved Simone out of the way. "Just let me holla at her real fast, and then me and you can finish this conversation. I promise."

She slowly walked over to her bed. "Its more than a conversation, but whatever. Just don't be with her all night. This is very important. I'm drowning here. I need you." She blinked and a tear slid down her cheek.

I nodded understandingly and opened the door.

As soon as it was open a little bit, Purity pushed it in and wrapped her arms around my neck, laying her head on my chest. "I'm tired, Shemar. I'm ready to go back to sleep. Ain't you been in here long enough?" she whined, before looking up into my eyes.

I shook my head, holding her. "Look, me and Simone just found out some serious news and we need to talk about it for a little while longer. After that, I'll be in there to hold you until you fall asleep. I promise." I moved her long hair out of her face, and tilted her chin upward so she could see the sincerity in my eyes.

Apart of me wanted to make her just go back in the room, but I knew that I couldn't be mean about it. My sister had been through a lot, and she needed me to take it easy on her feelings and emotions. She was broken, and only I could fix her. It wouldn't have helped matters any for me to further break her down. I was all that she had left now.

She nodded. "Okay, but is it going to take a long, long time, or will you be in there with me in like ten minutes?" She blinked a few times, looking like a vulnerable little girl. It made my heart flutter. I loved my lil' sister, man. She was my heart of hearts.

Simone jumped out of the bed and frowned. "Damn, Purity, he'll be in there in a minute. You can't be a hog all the time. I need him sometimes too. Don't you know that before you got here, everything that you two are doing we used to do, and now that you're here, we don't anymore, and it sucks." She frowned and mugged Purity with hatred.

Purity stepped away from me and into Simone's face. "Look, Simone, I don't give a care about nothin' you're saying. I haven't had my brother for over eight years, and he's my blood. I miss him, and I need him way more than you do. At least you have a mother and a father you can go to at any time. All I have is him, and I'm going to continue to hog him. So, step off, or step up. It's your choice, but I'm not afraid of you."

Simone lowered her eyes and bumped her forehead against Purity's, balling her hands into fists. "Whatever you wanna do, Purity, is cool with me. I'll fight for him because he's just as much my brother as he is yours, and you need to get that through your head."

Purity shook her head again and again. "No, he's not. No, he's not. No, he's not!" She pushed Simone so hard that she flew backwards and into the dresser, knocking off some of her hair care products to the floor. "He's not your brother, Simone! He's only mine, and I will kill you over him!" Purity's face turned bright red, both of her hands were balled into fists, and she looked like she was going to go psycho in any minute, had I not stepped in and pulled her back.

I wrapped my arms around her chest while she stood with her back to me. "Purity, what's wrong with you, lil' sis? Don't you know that we all are a family and we gotta get along? Huh?"

Simone slowly started to get up, holding her stomach. "Geez, Purity, it's not that serious. You could have really hurt me just now." She made her way to her feet and took three steps back, still holding her stomach.

Purity shook her head as if she was trying to knock herself out of the fog she had been in. "I'm sorry, Simone. I didn't mean it. I really didn't. I just love Shemar so much, but I'll go. I'll let you two talk." She attempted to walk over to Simone to console her, I imagined, but decided against it. Instead, she turned around to face me. "Can you please come to me soon? I want you to hold me for a little." She stepped on her tippy toes and kissed my cheek, before closing the door behind her.

I didn't even get a chance to give her my answer.

Simone rushed across the floor and locked the door. "That girl is crazy, and something isn't right. I need you to be honest with me, Shemar. Are you fucking her sometimes?" She turned her head to the side, awaiting my answer.

I felt beyond offended. I mean Purity was my little sister, and I know that me and Simone were claiming to be related, but in all actuality, we were not. There was no blood going through us that was the same. I was free to do to her whatever I wanted to. Whereas with Purity, I could not. "N'all, Simone. Me and my little sister ain't never went there, and that shit ain't ever crossed my mind. That's my blood. Have you forgot that?"

She shrugged. "That blood shit don't mean nothin'. Boy, we are in Houston. Everybody screwing somebody that they ain't supposed to. And far as that never crossing yo' mind, I can bet you a million dollars that it crossed hers on more than one occasion. I'm a female and I see the way she looks at you, and it ain't like no brother. She looks at you like you're her savior. Like you're the finest man in the world, and like you belong to her. That scares me, because we're going to have a child together. What does her being in the picture look like? Shit, what does it look like when she finds out?"

I exhaled loudly and grabbed her hand, pulling her to me, where I wrapped her into my big arms and held her close. "Look, Simone, we gon' figure this thing out for our child's sake. I love you, and I got you one hundred percent. You don't have to worry about nothing. Now that you have my seed growing inside of you, you are my first priority. I'm gon' make sure that I take care of all of them cravings that's finna take place. Be at all of the doctor appointments, and be there for you in any way that you need for me to be, emotionally and physically. I just gotta get my bread right, and I got less than nine months to do it. Do you trust me?"

She nodded. "Yeah, I do. I'm just scared, that's all. What do we tell our mother about this? And when?"

Chapter 6

I didn't want to waste no time with none of this, so an hour later, I woke up our mother and had her and Purity come to the living room, where they sat on the couch and watched us as we stood before them. The sun had not made its way up, and the house held an eerie silence until I spoke up and got the ball rolling, so to speak.

"Look, I hate to wake you up, momma, and you too Purity, but I gotta let this family know what's going on because we can't keep secrets from each other. I love all of y'all way too much to get down like that. So, with that being said, momma, Simone is pregnant. It's my child, and I'm finna stand up and be a man to make sure that she or our child don't need for nothin'. I got this. I just need for you to trust me."

My mother put her hand over her heart and bugged her eyes out of her head. "Pregnant?" she whispered in disbelief.

Purity stood up with her face scrunched. "Pregnant? Her? Yeah, right. How do you even know it's your kid? Have you taken a DNA test yet?" she asked, mugging the shit out of Simone.

Simone curled her upper lip. "It's too early for all of that, Purity. Why don't you stay in your place? We got this, over here." She rolled her eyes and turned her attention to our mother.

She stood up. "Shemar, I need to talk to you in the other room, right now." I watched my mother storm out of the living room. "Now Shemar!"

I was on my way to following her when Purity blocked my path. "Shemar, this don't mean that you love her more than me, do it? You're not going to leave me again, are you?"

I shook my head. "Purity, you're overreacting. Just wait for me in the room. I'll be in there in a minute." I walked past her and followed my mother into her room, where she closed the door behind me.

I walked over and sat on her bed. I already knew that she was finna tear into my ass. I was preparing for it. I felt like I had betrayed her in a sense, even though she had given me and Simone permission to mess around. I put both of my hands over my face and rubbed it. I was so exhausted.

She walked over to me and stood in front of me for a long time without saying a word. Out of nowhere, she grabbed my hand and pulled me up until I was towering over her, before she reached up and stroked my face. "You're my baby boy. Mommy's everything. I want you to know that I'm not mad at you, that I'm actually happy because it means that you'll be apart of this family for a long, long time. I knew what would happen once you kids got to doing your thing, and I prepared myself for this, mentally. I just want you to know that you belong to me, first. That you're my little man, no matter how big you get. You will always be mommy's little man, and I should always be your first." She kissed my lips, sucking them, while running her hands all over my back. Then, she leaned down and sucked on my stomach muscles, licking along my waistline. "Umm. I'm so glad that you'll be around for a long time." She stood back up and hugged me for a while.

I had so many thoughts going through my mind that I couldn't get a clear one to form itself. I was all over the place. The most reoccurring thought was that I needed to get money. I had to get my chips all the way up and break into Cloverland, now that Sherm was gon' and I had a child on the way. I would figure everything else out along the way. But the key to all of my so-called problems was chasing money. I hugged my mother real tight, then tongued her down for two whole minutes while she moaned into my mouth and ground her hips into me sensually.

After we broke the kiss, I kissed her neck. "I got this, momma. I gotta get my money right, and I need you to help me in any way that you can."

She nodded and rubbed my chest. "I'll do anything, baby. Just tell momma what you need, then do me real hard while I bite on the pillow. I need to feel you inside of me." She bit into my chest and moaned. "Ummm-a. My baby."

I sat her on the bed and kneeled. "I need you to come up with at least a hundred gees so I can hit this game running out here in Cloverland. I know Vincent got that ducked off somewhere, don't he?" Vincent was the Pastor's name, and though they were legally separated, I knew that she still handled all of the books for the church, and a few other nonprofit organizations that he had. I didn't know all of the logistics, but I knew she could get her hands on the money.

She pulled me to her by my waist, then she leaned forward and kissed my stomach. She rubbed all over it before sticking her hand down my boxers and squeezing my dick, stroking it. "Yeah, he does, but if I get that for you, baby, where does that leave us? Are you trying to get enough money to move away from me? Please say no." She pulled my dick all the way out and sucked the head into her mouth with her eyes closed. Her cheeks were hollowed out with her nose flared.

I watched her for a few seconds with my toes curling, loving the feel of her mouth. When it came to sucking me, my mother was a magician. I got to making noises right away and everything. "Huh! Huh! Huh! N'all, ma. I'll never leave you. I love you too much. I swear I do."

As crazy as it may sound, apart of me meant that a lil' bit. Ever since I had been a lil' kid, she had been all that I'd known. I was low key addicted to her. I couldn't imagine her not being a constant in my life. Then, the things she did to my body whenever she was given the chance to do them, kept me even more addicted to her. There was nothing like that real grown pussy to me. I was obsessed with it.

Her head went back and forth, faster and faster. She tightened her lips and started to moan real loud around my pipe. The noises were driving me crazy. I didn't know how much longer I could hold out.

She stuck her hand between her legs, then brought her fingers up to my nose, popping my dick out of her mouth. "Taste me, baby. Taste mommy. You remember what I taught you? If you can fall in love with mommy's taste, then you will never leave her. We will never be separated." She put her fingers on my lips and I sucked them into my mouth, hungrily.

I was sucking all over them and licking in between the cracks. She'd been doing that to me ever since I was too little to remember, and even back then, it drove me crazy. It was because of her that I was insane over the taste of pussy.

I stood up, picked her up and threw her on the bed. On my beast mode shit, I grabbed her gown by the collar and ripped it down the middle. She had me so riled up. "Momma, grab that pillow right there and be quiet. I'm finna kill this pussy. You hear me?" I asked through clenched teeth. I didn't even wait for her response.

She reached over and grabbed it, sticking a corner in her mouth and biting down on it, while I pushed her knees to her chest. Afterward, I took my dick and stuffed it into her wet hole like a savage. Her lips opened to accommodate me, then her walls were sucking at me as my dick went in and out of her at full speed. Her eyes were closed, and on her face was a frown.

"Hmm. Hmm. Hmm. Hmm. Uhh! Hmm. Hmm. Hmm Uhh! Hmmmmm-a!" She moaned over and over again while I tried to kill that pussy.

It was so wet and hot. Her nipples poked through the gown and looked like they were trying to come through the fabric. I leaned my head down and sucked them through the fabric, while my hips went as fast as they ever had. I needed to cum in her. I needed to feel my seed splashing against her walls. I was dying to feel that.

She continued to moan, then pulled down her shoulder straps, exposing her pretty brown titties. She squeezed them together, then grabbed me by the back of the head to pull me down to them so I could suck them like I was starving for milk. They were hard and rubbery, and the harder I sucked on them, the wetter her pussy got, until she started to shake and growl while biting on the pillow.

"Hrrr. Hrrr. Ummm. Hrrr. Umm. Umm. Huh. Huh. Ummm. Uhhhhhhh-a!" Her body started to shake like crazy, and I kept on pounding that pussy out with anger and lust.

I felt my seed building up deep inside of me. I stroked faster, hitting it harder, gritting my teeth together, and then I couldn't take it no more. I saw the look of ecstasy and pain on her face. The way her titties were jiggling with the hard nipples, the smell of her scent in the air— it was all too much. The next thing I knew, I was cumming harder than I ever had before, over and over again, deep within her hot ass womb, and it felt so good.

Afterward, we would lay on our sides while I slow-stroked her until the wee hours of the morning. She told me how she was going to get the money for me, ASAP. All I could do was smile because I knew I was finna get on my grind. I just didn't have all of the pieces of the puzzle together just yet.

As crazy as it may sound, the game kinda came to me before I could do my own thing to break into it.

Two days after I found out that I had Simone pregnant, Nikki called me and said that she needed me to come and pick her up from the hospital because she was being discharged, and that was music to my ears because I had missed her presence so much. As soon as I hung up the phone, I got dressed and shot right over to the hospital, where she was waiting on me, sitting in a wheel chair just inside of the sliding doors.

When she saw me, she wheeled herself out, and then jumped up from the chair and hugged me. "Damn, Shemar, I can't believe you let me wheel my own self out of the hospital. I guess you done changed since I been laid up, huh?" She looked up at me with a smile on her face.

I kissed her on the forehead and helped her to the car, closing the passenger door after she got in, then jogged around to the driver's side, and pulled off before I could even close the door. I hated hospitals, and I wanted to get as far away from that one as possible.

It was a bright and sunny day. A lil' humid, and I was just happy that Nikki was back beside me. I turned to look her over and peeped that she was eyeing me closely. "Why you looking at me like that?" I asked, smiling.

She squinted. "You just got done fuckin didn't you?"

I cocked my head back and laughed. "What make you say that, Nikki?" She always had this crazy way about reading me like nobody else could.

She shook her head. "N'all, nigga, answer my question, first. Did you just get done fuckin' or not? Don't make me go in yo' boxers and smell yo' shit for myself."

She had never done nothing like that before, so I knew she was playing. I still was gon' keep it one hundred with her. The whole time we had been friends, I had never told her one lie, and I intended to keep it that way.

I turned on to the highway and increased my speed, pulling past a blue minivan full of niggas. I nodded. "Yeah, I been fuckin all night. I'm tired as hell a lil' bit, but never the less, I'm happy to see you. We got plenty shit to discuss. It's time to get this money."

She nodded. "Okay. Okay. That sound good. I'm down with that. But my question to you is, who was you fuckin', because I was hitting yo' phone all morning, and you just now answering it. So, who is this bitch that got you putting me on hold?" She frowned and curled her upper lip. I could tell that she was heated.

For the first time, I wanted to spin her ass and not let her know who I had been laid up with. For as long as we had been cool, she had never known that I was fuckin' my foster mother. It's not that I would have lied to her about it had she asked, it's just that it never came up and I never volunteered the information.

"That's just my bad. I ain't have my phone on, period. It ain't got nothin' to do with who I was laid up with. I don't put no broad before you. Never have, never will. You know better than that."

She pursed her lips and took her long hair up into a pony tail, after letting her window down a lil' bit. "I can't tell. Had you been laid up in the hospital, the last thing on my mind would have been pussy. I would have been going crazy over worrying about you, and I would have been by your side every second of the day. And you still didn't tell me who this bitch was. So, who is she?"

I was going over her comments in my head and I felt like she had stabbed me in the heart with a knife.

It seemed to me that she was feeling like I had not been there for her the way that she needed me to be, and if that was the case, then I was about to be sick as hell because I knew that I would do anything for Nikki, including falling on a sword for her.

As I pulled in front of a big semi-truck on the highway, I turned to her and looked into her eyes. "You feel like I wasn't there for you when you was in there? Keep that shit gangsta with me." I was trying my best to not let on that I was softly dying inside.

She shook her head and waved me off, before messing with the radio. "Look, let's not get into that shit. That's behind us right now. Let's move forward." While she said this, I noted that she refused to make eye contact with me. "I wanna hear some Yo Gotti. That nigga always make me feel better." She started one of his tracks and let her seat all the way back, bobbing her head in silence.

I shook my head. "Nikki, what? You scared or somethin'? You scared to tell me how you really feel? Them slugs done made yo' ass soft? You pussy now?" I didn't mean to be disrespectful to her, but that was the only way I would be able to get her to speak on how she really felt in regards to me. I had to geek her up, and she hated when I called her soft or a pussy. So, I skated along those lines to get her to open up.

She clenched her jaw and mugged me. "Shemar, just quit while you ahead, nigga, fa real, 'cause you blowing me right now. Don't ask for the truth if you can't handle that shit. I'm telling you now." She flared her nostrils and looked out of the window.

I pushed her thick left thigh and curled my lip. "Whatever, nigga, you just soft now. I'm finna drop yo' ass off 'cause I ain't tryna be around this new version of you. This shit weak."

She shot daggers at me. "You wanna do this shit, nigga? Huh? You really want me to go there?"

I nodded. "Yeah, I really do. I can handle it. Ain't shit soft about me. I need that shit uncut at all times. You playin' pussy enough for the both of us." I looked out of my windshield as a dude on a Ducatti drove in front of my whip without a helmet on. He stayed in that spot for a short second, then drove into the right lane, weaving in and out of traffic.

"Awright, Shemar, just keeping shit real. N'all, nigga, you wasn't there for me the way that you should have been. I was needing you while I was laid up in that hospital, and you came and saw me maybe three times. Every time I opened my eyes, I was expecting to see your face, but I didn't, and that shit killed my soul because you're supposed to have my back until the bitter end. You're all the family that I really have. Then, when it's time for me leave today, instead of you picking up on the first ring, you don't pick your phone up until three hours later, because you was laid up with this secret bitch whose name you won't even tell me. It's like, damn, I been out of the picture for a short while and already you shitting on me. I feel like killing somethin' and breaking down crying at the same time. I don't know what to do." She looked back out the window, reached and turned up the music.

I felt like the worst bitch ass nigga in the whole wide world. Man, Nikki had my soul. We had been through so much together that I would seriously rather be dead than to not have her in my life. Just thinking about me dropping the ball with her situation made me want to blow my own brains out. I didn't even know that I had failed her until she said it.

I reached and turned down the music, then put my hand on her knee. "Nikki, I'm sorry, ma. You know that I love yo' ass like crazy, and I didn't mean to drop the ball like I did. It's just so much shit done took place ever since you been down. I been hunting the niggas that did this shit to you, and bodied they ass. I had to knock off the Deacon and a few members of his family because I found out they were molesting my sister. Then, I just found out that Simone pregnant by me. My sister lives with us now, and my foster mother separated from the Pastor. So, it's all kind of drama that been taking place. On top of that, them Pigs been all over the hood, sweating us like crazy."

She nodded slowly. "So, Simone the reason you ain't pick yo' phone up when I called? And you got this bitch pregnant?" She sucked her teeth loudly. "I know you ain't finna let her keep that." She scrunched her face and looked highly upset.

Out of all the shit I had just said to her, that was the only one she wanted to comment on. That through me for a loop. "Really? That's all you heard out of everything I just said to you?"

She shook her head. "N'all, I heard everything and I'll get to them in a minute. Right now, I wanna know what you finna do with this bitch's baby, because if we finna be getting money, ain't neither one of us got no time to be having no kids. I thought we already talked about that shit, didn't we?"

I kept driving, looking straight ahead and trying to keep my cool. Nikki was everything to me, but I hated when she tried to impose too deeply into my personal life. I wanted to check her ass but, once again, I knew that wouldn't have been appropriate.

She dug her nails into my thigh. "Nigga, I know you hear me talkin' to yo' ass. You said that neither one of us would have a child until we had at least a mill in the bank apiece, and the only way a child would come before then is if we had one together. Seeing as we never fucked, and wasn't fucking before I got hit with them slugs, the odds of that happening was zero to none." She balled her hands into fists and slammed them down on the side of her. "Damn, you got that bitch pregnant! Is this the bitch that had you miss my calls this morning!" She reached over and grabbed my chin, forcing me to look at her. I guess she didn't care if we crashed, so I didn't either.

I exhaled. "N'all, Nikki, I was fucking the Pastor's wife this morning, and my phone was in my pants, under the bed. That's why I didn't hear your calls."

She pushed my face away from her. "Damn, so you fuckin' both of them bitches? Since when, Shemar? How long you been gettin' down with them?"

I pulled all the way over to the right lane and got off on the exit ramp. I was hungry as hell and I knew that I needed to put some food in Nikki's stomach. She looked like she had lost about ten pounds since she'd taken them slugs. I didn't like her looking all skinny and shit.

"I been fuckin' my foster mother since I was about thirteen, and Simone since seventeen."

Nikki's eyes got bucked. "Thirteen? You been fuckin' that bitch since you was thirteen, and you never told me?" She jerked her head back. "Wow, ain't that a bitch? Here I am thinking that I knew you inside-out, and come to find out that you ain't even the nigga that I thought you was. Fuck you breaking my heart. On my dead father, you let that bitch have yo' baby and I'm killing you and her. I ain't with that shit. I don't know what all been goin' on since I been out of commission, but I'm still yo' right hand nigga, and we still eat out these slums together. I ain't sharing you with no baby, plus you ain't ready fo' that shit no way. You ain't got a mill yet, do you?"

I shook my head. "N'all, I don't, but I'm finna get it." I wanted to tell her that I was ready to have a child. That I would do whatever it took for my child when it got here. That I would hold Simone down one hundred percent, but I knew that it would all fall on deaf ears. Plus, I didn't really know what I wanted at that time.

Mentally, I was going through it on all levels because so many people needed me, and I had to make sure that they were all secure.

I pulled into the Jack in the Box parking lot and thought about going through the drive thru, but the line was long and damn near in the street. So, I decided that we'd just eat inside. I parked my whip and turned off the ignition, along with the music.

Nikki had been bobbing her head, but once the music stopped, all she did was mug me.

"You finna put some food in yo stomach. I don't care what you say."

She sat back and crossed her arms over her breasts. "Shit, I ain't finna argue with you. Long as you paying, I'll eat everything they got in that muhfucka, and you probably will too, since you been fucking mothers and daughters and shit. Damn, them bitches done took my nigga from me." She lowered her head and shook it.

I was about to tell her that she was overreacting when something told me to look to my left, and I did. I reached under my seat to grab my Tech .9, but they had the ups on me. The blue minivan that I had passed on the highway pulled up alongside of my whip, and about ten niggas jumped out with black ski masks over their faces and AK47's in their hands.

One of them stuck his gun through the window and pressed it to the back of my head. "Look, nigga, if you move, I'm splashing you and that bitch. My chief wanna see you in person. All this is, is a meeting. Don't turn this shit into a homicide, because that ain't no thang, man."

I heard him opening my car door, and Nikki being pulled out of the passenger's seat. The only thing I could imagine were our funerals.

Chapter 7

I didn't know where the fuck we were at the time. I wouldn't find it out until later that me and Nikki had been taken into the sewer system under Cloverland. All I knew was that it smelled horrible. It was dark and rank down there, and they had us blindfolded the whole time. I felt myself being slammed into a chair, and then my blindfold was ripped off. I was able to see a dim light off in the distance. Nikki was beside me. In front and behind us were about twenty niggas, all heavily armed, with black ski masks over their faces. Their arms were huge like they worked out every single day. They reminded me of army men. My stomach was in knots. I feared more for Nikki than myself because she had already been through so much, and I knew that often in hostage situations that most fuck niggas liked to rape the women before they killed them. I would make them bitch niggas kill me first before I allowed that. I had failed her enough.

We sat there for what felt like three hours in silence with guns pointed at us, though it must have only been about thirty minutes, when a caramel skinned nigga pulled up on a four-wheeler with half of black mask covering his face. On the back of the four-wheeler was a female whose face was also covered part way.

He got off of it and stood up, helping her off of it as well, before they walked over to me. He looked down at her. "Is this the nigga right here, baby? Look at him real close, now."

I looked up to her and saw that her eyes were very familiar. She looked at me for a long time, looking deep into my eyes as if she were trying to look into the deepest pits of my soul.

She squinted, then reached and took the side of my face in her hand, before nodding her head. "Yeah, Pops, this him." Then, she took a step back and the caramel nigga stepped up to me with a mug on his face.

I was braced myself, expecting him to lash out and hit me or something. I couldn't place the face of the female, though I knew that as long as I had been hitting licks that I had never hurt one.

The dude kneeled and pulled the mask off of his face. "Do you know who I am, lil' nigga? Huh?"

I shook my head. I had never seen him before in my life. Once again, I was hoping that my past wasn't coming back to haunt me. If it was, I just wanted them to let Nikki go. "Look, homie. Whatever I did to you, she ain't have nothin' to do with it. Take that shit out on me and I'll take my punishment as a man."

He laughed, and looked over his shoulder at all of his niggas that were heavily armed, before looking back at me. "You killed my nigga Sherm the other night, and a few other niggas. Then, you and her over there hit another one of my workers, and bodied three of them. So, when you say that she ain't got nothin' to do with none of this, that ain't the truth because she just as guilty."

Nikki mugged him. "You muthafuckin' right. Anything that you gon' do to him, you gon' do to me too. That's my nigga, and we in this shit together, for life. Fuck all them niggas you just named. If they dead, let they bitch ass rest in peace." She spat on the ground. "Yo', Shemar, don't play me like that. I don't need no favors. We in this shit together. Loyalty in blood, nigga. You already know that."

I exhaled and closed my eyes for a brief second. I didn't want them putting they hands on her. I would have rather died for the both of us.

The female walked over and placed her hand on my shoulder. "That's yo' girl or somethin'? Why she screaming death beside you like that?" She looked over to Nikki and raised her eyebrow.

I nodded. "That's my heart. She ain't my woman. She more than that. Once again, this shit ain't got nothin' to do with her. Put that bullet in my head and let me pay for our sins against yo' niggas. They done already put slugs in her back. It's my turn."

The nigga stood up and looked down at me. "You must really not know why you here, lil' homie." He looked over to the masked female. "Baby, take that shit off of yo' face so he can see who you is. Then, we can move on with this project."

The female took a step back and pulled her mask off of her face, then slowly walked toward me with the lights flickering on and off behind her. "Don't you remember me, now? Huh? The other day, when you and yo' niggas hit up Sherm, instead of you allowing them to kill, me you told me to get behind the couch while y'all handled y'all business. Three other girls got killed that night, but you spared my life, and I know that you didn't have nothin' to do with them being killed either." She came and kneeled in front of me, grabbing my hand. "This my father, Taurus. My name is Jahliya. Because of what you've done, my old man owes you a favor, and I feel like I owe you my life. So, don't worry about nobody hurting you or her, because that ain't gon' happen."

I bugged my eyes out of my head and I couldn't believe everything that was taking place. I hadn't even thought about the female that I had made get behind the couch, so I could spare her life. Now, here she was, alive and well and doing the same for me.

I took a deep breath and looked over at Nikki whose eyes were open so wide that her forehead had wrinkles all over it. "Look, Jahliya, that move ain't have nothin' to do with you or them other girls. If it was up to me, I wouldn't have let nothing happen to neither one of them, but that situation got out of control. But you right, I ain't have nothin' to do with them being killed, and that don't mean that I'm gon' run my mouth about who did. My only concern is her, over there. Whatever business y'all gotta handle with me, why don't y'all let her go first, then we can do whatever."

Nikki tried to stand up, but one of the beefy dudes slammed her back into her seat. After she sat back down, she looked up at him with a mug on her face before turning to me. "Man, Shemar, stop sayin' that shit. Whatever they finna do to you, they finna do to me, too. Nigga, we bleed together, so fuck that soft shit you on right now."

Jahliya shook her head. "Ain't nobody on nothin' with him. Now, it's unfortunate that them other broads got stanked, but still in all, he saved my life, and he ain't have nothin' to do with that. The reason I had him snatched up is because my family owes him a favor. The way my old man get down, he gon' make sure that he bless any nigga that look out for somebody of our bloodline. So, y'all in good hands. Stop freaking out." She looked over to Taurus. "Pops."

He waved his hand through the air, and one by one, all of the big muscle-bound dudes started to leave the area in which we were, until all that was left was me, Nikki, Taurus and Jahliya. Taurus grabbed a chair and sat it down a few feet in front of me, then he stared at me for a long time without saying a word.

Jahliya had a worried look on her face. "Dad, why you ain't sayin' nothin'?" She came and stood beside him, mugging the side of his head.

Taurus curled his upper lip and sucked his teeth, shaking his head without saying a word. He laughed, looked up at her and then back to me. "I lost over two hundred thousand dollars for that lick that y'all hit with Bryan. I'm paying Mickey's hospital bills right now, because I can't afford for this bitch nigga to turn State against my organization. Five murders in less than a month— all of them are somehow connected to my organization, one way or the other, and because you saved my daughter's life I can't do nothin' about that." He laughed and shook his head. "Nigga, I'm down a total of five hundred gees and the Feds are all over me, right now, along with the local authorities. But since you saved my daughter's life, I gotta overlook all of this shit that I got crashing down on me, and I just gotta figure it all out before it crushes my shoulders." He sucked his teeth and stood up, slamming the metal chair so hard to the ground that it bent in half. Then, he began to pace while Jahliya kneeled on the side of me and put her hand on my knee.

I looked over at Nikki and her eyes were on Jahliya's hand as if she wanted to cut that muhfucka off. I mean, she frowned and I had never seen that look on her face in regards to me before. Taurus' pacing was getting me antsy. I'd heard everything that he was saying and it made me paranoid because he knew too much, and I didn't know that them people were coming at him for the shit that I'd done. I also didn't know that he was the man behind the man. I got to thinking about how easy it was for him to find me, and I wondered why he had not found me sooner and handled his business. I felt Jahliya squeeze my knee, and that made me look down into her light brown eyes. She smiled at me nervously, then looked up at her father as he stopped pacing in front of me, and pulled her up by her arm.

"Baby, take her, and y'all wait outside for us. I need to holla at him like a man on some real shit."
Jahliya frowned and looked like she was about to protest, until Taurus gave her a look that said he meant business. He lowered his eyes and scrunched his face. That made her eyes get big.

She nodded and backed toward Nikki. "Come on. They'll be out in a minute."

Nikki stood up and shook her head. "N'all, fuck that. I ain't going nowhere. That's my homie, right there. What yo' Pops finna do to him that I need to step out of the room for?" she asked, walking toward me.

Taurus looked down at me. "Say, lil' homie, talk to yo' people, man, and tell shawty it's all good. We need to get an understandin' between us. Now, I'm being as civil as I possibly can. You'll never see me this humble again. Trust me." He lowered his eyes and clenched his teeth.

There was something about his stare that screamed death. Just by me being in the slums ever since I was a kid, I could tell that this nigga wasn't the one to play with. I felt like Nikki was pressing her luck, and I couldn't risk something happening to her.

I stood up and walked over to Nikki, putting my hands on her shoulders. "Look, ma, let me holla at this nigga real quick. If somethin' was gon' happen, I'm pretty sure it would have already. We done fucked him over a lot, and now as a man, I gotta hear him out. Just go with Jahliya and I'll be right behind you in a minute. Okay?"

She looked up at me, frowning. Her pretty face was all scrunched together. After not saying a word and our eyes searching each other's, she exhaled loudly. "Damn. Okay, Shemar, but I don't like this shit. Everything we do, we supposed to do it together. What if homie put a bullet in yo' head once I leave this dungeon? Then what?" She stepped to the side of me and hollered at Taurus. "Say, my nigga, if you put a bullet in his head once I leave this room, you just make sure that you put one in my head in the same place as the one in my nigga's. Fuck life if he ain't here with me." She kissed me on the cheek, and her and Jahliya disappeared through the big metal door that we had come through.

After they were gone, Taurus opened his hand and pointed at the chair I was sitting in. I took his cue and sat in it. He sat in the chair that Nikki had been sitting in, after pulling it closer to mine. He was less than four feet away from me.

He leaned closer, almost in my face, and mugged the shit out of me. "Nigga, you lucky you saved my daughter's life, because I was one day away from killing you and yo' whole family that stay over there on Roosevelt Drive. Fuck nigga, you know how much money you cost me in the last month? Huh? Like I said, half a million. Now, I know you ain't got that kind of scratch, because if you did, you wouldn't be out here pullin' these petty, hustlin' ass kick-doe's. I want you in a body bag, nigga. That's just me being honest." He was frowning so hard that his left eye was twitching.

I was trying my best to not look this nigga in the face, because if I did, I knew I was gon' buss him in his shit with all of my might. The way I saw it, there was nobody else around. It was just me and him. Even though he was a big, cocky nigga, I didn't give a fuck. He was gon' have to kill me in there. I was no lil' nigga either. I was gon' go for what I knew.

"So, what you saying, nigga? All you gotta do is let Nikki go, and we can do whatever is on yo' mind. I promise you that death talk ain't scaring me. I'm stressed the fuck out, and I got a bunch of people eating off of my plate. So, I'm gon' keep on hittin' these bitch niggas in Cloverland until I get the key to the streets. Fuck what you lost. It's part of the game, Taurus. So, what, nigga?" Now, I was looking this nigga in his eyes and ready to rush his bitch ass.

Taurus flared his nostrils and kept his eyes pinned on me. His eye continued to twitch. He smiled all evil-like, and ran his thumb and index finger along his goatee. "As much as I wanna kill you, lil' nigga, I gotta honor yo' gangsta because a lesser man in your position would fold. But you holding yo' own, and that girl out there got just as much heart as you do. Y'all remind me of me and my wife." He scooted his seat back and stood up, wiggling a finger in his ear. "You owe me five hundred gees, nigga, and I'm gon' get my money, one way or the other, but I got a proposition for you. I'm not just doing this because you saved my lil' girl's life, but also because I see a lot of me in you, and I can tell that you hungry. I peeped out yo' whole lil' situation, and I see that it's all females that's eating off of yo' plate. They depend on you to make a way, no matter how you have to, just as long as you do. I been there before, lil' homie, and it's for you to protect those women. Unfortunately, if you don't take this proposition, I promise you ain't gon' be able to do that. Now, it's true that you saved my daughter's life. So, that just means that I'ma spare yours this time. But just yours. All those other lives that represent you are up for grabs." He smiled, then frowned again. "You understanding me, right now?"

I stood up and lowered my eyes. I ain't ever had no nigga threaten my people before without me knocking they head off of their shoulders. Had I had any type of pistol with me, I would have emptied that bitch all in Taurus' face. That shit made me smile as I mentally saw each hole fill his shit up. "What's the proposition?" I asked, feeling my heart beat rapidly in my chest.

He picked a piece of lint off of his pants and flicked it, then dusted them off. I noted that he had on some fresh beige Timbs, and the shoe strings were loose. "I want you to work for me, and I'ma help you get rich, as long as you follow my game plan. I'ma take twenty-five percent of everything you make weekly until my five hundred gees is paid back. Seventy-five percent of everything you make will be yours, and I'ma sell you the dope wholesale. I ain't talking that shit that been stepped on more than a door mat. N'all. I'm talking first-class heroin, I'm the master of the Rebirth."

I lowered my head for a second, frowning, then I looked back up at him because I had heard about the Rebirth Heroin. It was supposed to be so addictive that the feens could not stay away from it once they shot it the first time. They said that with the Rebirth, it was like you was getting high for the first time, every time. I'd heard that they were traveling all the way to Memphis just to get it.

Now the name Taurus was ringing a bell to me, but I still had to confirm some things. "You from Memphis, homie?"

He nodded. "By way of Chicago, lil' nigga, and if you trying to find out if I'm that nigga, then let me just tell you right now, I'm that nigga." He spat on the concrete. "Fuck with me and I'll get you rich, but you gon' pay me my money back along the way."

I rubbed my chin and looked at the ground. "All I care about is feeding my people, and getting my piece of Cloverland. I been here since I was a young'in. This where my heart is. I'ma die right here with a smile on my face. So, if I'm hustlin' fa' you, I want my piece of these slums. Let me get the slot that Sherm had."

Taurus laughed. "I like you, lil' nigga, on some real shit." He shrugged. "I ain't ever liked that nigga Sherm no way. What happened is behind us now, and I wish it was that easy for me to just give you his slot, but it don't work like that. He got two niggas that worked under him that want his old slot. In order for you to sit on the throne of Cloverland that he used to, you gotta knock them niggas off in a bloody fashion to make a statement to the rest of the slums, that you ain't to be fucked with or stepped on, and that you in this game now, so muhfuckas gotta honor yo' slot. One thing I don't like about Houston is that it's too grimy out here. Too many cut throats. Ain't no loyalty, which is why I'm barely out this way. However, you were bred by these slums, so this shit in you."

I curled my upper lip and wiped my mouth. "You damn right, it's in me, and I'll die for these slums. It's all I know. Far as you speaking on them two niggas, give me the blueprints and I'll handle my business. After it's all said and done, I'll pledge my loyalty to you in blood."

Taurus nodded. "Before any of this take place though, you gotta finish that nigga Mickey. We can't begin somethin' new with unfinished business. Shit don't work like that. So, finish him, and then we can move forward. I'll have everything that you need after you make that statement to me through the death of him."

I walked forward and held my hand out. I don't know why I did it. I was just so excited to get the nod from him. I wanted to conquer my slums so bad. I wanted feed the young, starvin' niggas that were under me. I wanted to build up a new breed of niggas that were insane with loyalty.

After our talk, the girls came back in. Nikki entered with a scowl. She walked right up to me and rubbed the side of my face. "You good, Shemar? Tell me that we gon' wet this nigga and his daughter later," she whispered so low that I could barely hear her.

All I could do was smile and shake my head.

Jahliya walked over to me and grabbed my hand, pulling me away from Nikki, even though it took a second or two before Nikki let my hand go. Once we were out of ear shot and standing under the flickering light with the spiders crawling all over it, she exhaled. "Shemar, I like you, and I thank you for saving my life. I hope you let me make it up to you by taking you to Hawaii with me this summer. I go every year alone, but this time I would be happy if you would accompany me. I know you'll have a good time." She smiled, showing off her deep dimples and pretty face. To say that I was mesmerized would have been an understatement. She put her hand on my chest. "You ain't gotta make yo' mind up right away. I'll be in touch. I got a few other things for you too, but, like I said before, I'll be in touch." She sucked on her bottom lip and looked me in the eyes. "Damn, your eyes are crazy. I could never forget them, nor would I ever have to. You'll see. I want you, and what I want, I get." She walked off, and Taurus put his arm around her neck as they stepped past the big metal door.

Nikki stepped up to me and mugged the shit out of Jahliya's back. "I already know you finna be fuckin' that bitch. Even though I'm a lil' worried, because I know you finna add her to all them other broads in the picture, I know you gon' make that bad ass bitch elevate us in the game, am I right?"

I put my arm around her and kissed her forehead. "You damn right."

Ghost

Chapter 8

"Yo, Kid, I can't believe we about to kill Sun in a hospital. I never knew you niggas got down like that out here. Word is bond," Nut said as he held the door to the men's restroom closed in Mount Sinai hospital.

I slipped my blue scrubs on that Nikki had somehow got me. They fit kinda snug, but I didn't even care because all I could think about was bodying that nigga Mickey and getting the fuck out of there. I slipped my Air Max back on and tied the strings. "That's what's wrong with you New York niggas. Y'all think y'all the only ones that's 'bout that life."

It was about 9PM and the hospital, for some reason, was busy as hell. They had Mickey up on the eighth floor where he was laid up from having complications with his colostomy bag. I didn't know what that meant, but I was finna make my next move my best move.

I had a big ass hunting knife on me like the ones the Pastor used when he took me hunting with him. It had a holster and everything. I was gone make a statement to Taurus to let that nigga know that this shit wasn't a game. I wanted in to Cloverland.

I had waited my whole life for it and I was willing to do anything, within reason to do so. I wished that we didn't have to wait damn near two hours to go up to Mickey's floor, but that wasn't the case. Due to the fact that there were so many orderlies around, me and Nut spent a lot of time ducking they ass and hiding in the restroom with our heads down like we were cleaning it. We had our sanitation stuff on, along with the blue masks that the doctors and janitors used to cover their nose and mouth. I even had the blue hat on my head to covered up my waves, and some big ass glasses that didn't have any prescription to them. The last thing I needed was to be identified by anybody.

When the time came for me to hit up Mickey, I crept down the hall that Nut was moping, and we made eye contact. He nodded in the direction of Mickey's room, and I took that as my cue to handle my business. I looked both ways and made sure the coast was clear before I grabbed the door handle with my gloved hand and twisted it, slipping into the room, closing the door behind me.

When I got inside, that fool Mickey was laying on his side with his back to the door. It smelled like shit in his room. I'll never forget that stench. I guessed he was sleep because he barely moved as I got closer and closer to the bed. I slipped the knife out of its holster on my waist, put my hand over his mouth, and stabbed him in the back again and again, while he struggled against me, screaming into my hand.

"Hrrrgh! Hrrrgh! Hmp! Hmp! Hmp! Hmp!" His body jerked violently.

I felt his hot blood splattering on my glove. The knife broke through his ribs and punctured his muscles and tissues. Blood oozed out of him in thick rivulets. I slammed the knife into him again and pulled it upward. He started to throw up blood into my gloved hand. I took a step back and looked him over. His bed was covered with his blood. It looked like a scary movie or something.

He turned around, reaching out to me. He tried to talk, but only coughed up a bloody loogey. I grabbed his forehead and commenced to stabbing him over and over again, killing him before slamming the knife into his heart and twisting it.

When I got back into the hallway, it was still quiet and Nut was moping the floor like nothing was going on. Once again, we made eye contact, and then got up out of there.

That night, I let the shower's water beat down on my face while I thought things through thoroughly. I had a whole lot on my plate, and it seemed like every time one thing was conquered, another sprung up. I had to find a way to get myself into a better, more stable position, so I could be able to provide for my child that was on the way, and my sister. I also needed to make sure that Nikki was straight on all levels. Just as bad as I wanted to have my piece of the slums, she wanted it too for herself. Well, more so for the both of us. I loved her, and I had to make sure that I held her down before somebody took my life. I felt like that was gon' happen soon, and I had to make sure shit was in order first.

I didn't really care about killing Mickey. To be honest, it felt good to me. Deep down within the pits of my soul, there was some evil there that I couldn't really explain nor understand, but it was a part of me.

I really didn't know how I felt about the nigga Taurus yet. I knew that I was gon' use him to break into the game, hard, and I was hoping that we could develop some sort of loyalty amongst each other. One things for sure, if he was helping me feed my family, then I was gon' ride for him until my common sense told me otherwise. On the low, I wanted the power that he had and I saw myself finding a way to get everything that he had. But first, I needed for him to trust me. Once I lowered his defenses, I could make my move.

This night, Purity knocked on the door, and then just came into the bathroom, locking the door behind her. The sudden sound of the door opening caught me off guard. You see, after a man gets so many murders under his belt, it causes every little noise to put you on high alert because you're always preparing for the karma that comes along with taking a life. You're always waiting on your time to pay the Reaper.

I moved back the curtain a little bit so I could stick my head out of it while the hot water continued to beat down on my back. The water was hot enough to cause the bathroom to steam up. "Purity, what you doing in here? Can't you see that I'm in the shower?"

She shrugged. "So, what? I need to talk to you, and I can't talk to you out there because one of them bitches always in yo' face, sucking up all yo' oxygen." She rolled her eyes. "I never did get the chance to ask you about this whole baby situation, so I'm doing it now, and please be honest with me. I need to know if her havin' yo' baby gon' make you love her more than me. I need to know where that leaves me and you, because I never factored in anybody else. I thought that when you turned eighteen, that it was just gon' be me and you for the rest of our lives." She swallowed, and I could tell that she was getting choked up.

I felt so uncomfortable talking to my sister ass naked that I figured I'd get myself together, then I would come out and holler at her in our room, like I normally did. "Look, Purity, I'm almost done in here. As soon as I finish up, why don't me and you close our bedroom door and we'll get an understanding about all of this?"

She nodded, and I pulled the curtain back so I could finish my shower.

Less than a minute passed before the curtain was pulled back and Purity was stepping into the shower, as naked as the day she came into the world. I looked her up and down before closing my eyes and trying to get those images out of my head of her.

One minute, the water was beating down on my chest, and the next thing I knew it stopped. I opened my eyes to see it raining down on her hair. She allowed for it to turn her natural hair into curls, running her fingers through it with her eyes closed. Below, her breasts jiggled every time she moved the slightest.

I frowned. "Purity, get yo' ass out this shower, right now. I ain't playin' with you."

She opened her eyes and blinked, taking her hands and wiping the water out of her face. "I ain't goin' nowhere. I need you to tell me how all of this is going to affect our relationship? I can't compete with her now that she has your kid. I know you gon' wind up lovin' her more than me now, and I can't handle that, Shemar. You're all that I have now, and the only thing I can offer you is what I have, and that's my body. So, please take it, because I can't lose you." She stepped forward and grabbed my piece, squeezing it in her hand, then kissed me on the neck.

I jerked my head back and slapped her hand away, stepping out of the shower and onto the shower mat. I couldn't believe my lil' sister. I grabbed the drying towel and started to dry my body. "Purity, you buggin' right now, lil' sis. I don't know what's the matter with you, but somethin' ain't right, and we need to talk about this, right now."

She turned off the shower and stepped out of the tub, stepping in front of me, reaching for my piece again and holding it. "All them bitches get to get some of my brother and I can't. That's bullshit. The only way you gon' wind up lovin' one of them more than me is because of them giving you some of the same cat that I got between my legs. Don't you see that you don't need none of them? You can have me. Ain't I just as pretty as Simone? Ain't we both the same height and weight? I even got more ass than she do. Look." She turned around and bent over the tub, pushing her ass into my lap, moving it from side to side.

I reached and grabbed her hip, pulling her up and pressing her against the wall, looking down at her. "Look, Purity, you my sister. You gotta get off of this bullshit. I'll never love anybody more than I love you. Everything I do in this world is for you, first. You are my angel; don't you understand that?" I rubbed her cheek, looking into her eyes as she blinked tears.

She shook her head. "I wanna believe that, Shemar, but what do I have to offer you? What's to stop you from leaving me like mommy and daddy did? Can't you see how much I need you at all times?" She whimpered, and snot dripped out of her nose before she sniffed it back up and swallowed.

I kissed her forehead. "Baby, it's okay. Just as much as you need me, I need you. Life don't make sense without you. We are all that we have. I get that, and I will never leave you, ever." Since I had gotten out of the water, now I was feeling a lil' hot, as if the heat was on too high. I felt my forehead perspiring.

Purity started to cry while I rubbed her cheek with my thumbs. "I want you to want me, Shemar, like you want Simone and Vicki. I want you to have me like you have them. It's the only way I can compete with them hoes." Tears continued to roll down her cheeks. She sniffed the snot back into her nostrils.

I shook my head slowly, looking down at her. She was breaking my heart. I didn't know that my sister was so broken. So afraid that I would leave her side for any reason at all. I tried to think of a million ways to console her. A million ways to let her know that I would never hurt her in that way. That I would rather die first. She was my angel— my purpose for breathing, and I meant that. "Purity, you are my sister. I could never want you like I want them, because I'm not supposed to. You're my heart, though. That's somethin' that neither one of them could ever be, because that place is reserved for you and only you, until my last breath."

She shook her head. "No. No. No. I know better. I know what it takes for a man to love a female. You gotta give them some pussy. It's the only way they'll want you. Just because you're my brother, Shemar, that doesn't make you any different. Sooner or later, you're going to love them more than me because they're giving you what you won't take from me. Now, I need you. Please." She reached under my towel and grabbed a hold of my pipe again, pumping it, before ripping my towel off of me.

When she dropped to her knees and kissed the head, I jumped back and smacked her hand away once again. She looked up at me with a look of confusion on her face.

"Purity, stop that shit, ma. Come on and get up." I helped her get to her feet, then I wrapped her into my arms, holding her to my chest while she cried and cried. "Sis, I love you, lil' momma, and you ain't ever gotta worry about nobody takin' yo' place because nobody can. I love you with all of my heart. I love you more than pussy, more than anything that is in this world, and you need to know that to be true. What you and I have, nobody can get in the way of that. Ever, baby. I promise."

She hugged me with all of her might and cried harder. "I want to die all the time, Shemar. I can't take it in this world thinkin' about you leavin' me every second of every day. And it doesn't matter what you say to me, I still don't think I'm enough, and I still feel like one day you're going to choose another female over me. Whether it be another female in this house, or out there in that world. Either way, it is going to kill me. It already is, and I can't take this shit anymore." She took a step back and looked up into my face. Hers was full of tears. "Why won't you just make love to me like you do them? What's so special about them that they get to have all of you and I don't? Is it because I already have somebody else's baby inside of me?" She blinked, and I could see that she was really hurting.

It made me feel lower than scum. I felt like I wanted to throw up or something, because for her to be behaving the way that she was meant that somebody had screwed my sister's head up, and clearly, I wasn't helping her enough. I was supposed to be her protector. I was supposed to make sure that she never reached harm. That was my job.

I looked into her beautiful face and I felt a tear slide down my cheek. "Damn, Purity. You hurting in there, baby, and I'm so sorry that I didn't see nor realize that sooner. I'll do anything for you. No one is more special to me than you are. No one. You're my sister. That's why I can't make love to you. It doesn't take for a female to sleep with a man in order for him to love her. That's bullshit, and it's some of the game that the Deacon and his family used on you in order to get you to do what they wanted. When it comes to me and you, I don't need you in that way to love you more than everybody else because you are my everything, and that will never change. You are special. You are my Diamond, and that's why I didn't hesitate to do what I had to do for you when it came to the Deacon and his sick ass family." I kissed her forehead again, and hugged her, feeling her wrap her little arms around me.

We hugged each other for about five minutes without saying a word, then she broke the silence. "Shemar?"

I held her more firmly with my mind all over the place. I was trying to figure out how I was going to heal my baby sister. I knew that she needed me, and

I had to find a way to be there for her on all levels. "Yeah, Purity?"

"Um, I know that you're not supposed to see me in that light. I can never trust none of them dudes out there, and I don't want them touching me, ever. Just thinking about it makes me sick on the stomach. However, I do have needs, now that I know what this sex thing is all about. I don't desire any male in this world but you. I heard Simone tell you a few times that I saw you in a way that I'm not supposed to, and even though I hate her guts, she's right. I want you in more ways than a brother. So, would it be so bad if, from time to time, you gave me some? I mean, if it was only between me and you? Huh?" She looked up at me once again with her big hazel eyes peering into mine.

I shook my head. "We can't get down like that, Purity. You my sister, and right now, you're just mentally broken. I'ma help you heal in any way that I can because you matter to me."

She bit her bottom lip, then sucked it. "But I want you to. I need your body, Shemar, and I'm the only one that's not getting it. It's not fair. I'm your angel; you said that." She reached between us and grabbed my pipe again, rubbing him all over her stomach. "Please? I'll do anything. Let's just keep it between me and you. It's plenty of my friends that done told me their secrets about stuff like that, but I'll never tell. I promise, I'll die if you say no." She whimpered.

I felt her pulling on him, and pressing him up against her naked stomach. My mind was everywhere but there. I was in a faraway zone, trying to make sense of things. My sister was broken. I felt like

I had dropped the ball in her protection. I didn't know what to do in that moment. I didn't know what to say. I wanted to be there for her in every single way, and at the same time smack her hand off of my pipe. I didn't know which thing would hurt her the most. I was so lost, and once again, I didn't come back to reality until I noted that she was rubbing me in between her sex lips and moaning. Only then did I take a step back and push her hand away.

She dropped to her knees with her hands covering her face, crying in emotional pain. "I don't have anything to offer you. I'm not good enough. You won't love me for too much longer. I just wanna die." She groaned and broke into a fit of coughs before sobbing uncontrollably.

I dropped to my knees and wrapped her in my arms. I held her close, kissing her tear-stained cheeks again and again, before rocking back and forth with her. "I love you, Purity, and I will never leave you. You mean the world to me. You're my angel; you're my everything." Over and over I said these things to her while I held her in my arms.

We cried on that floor together for the next hour, until she grew tired. Then, I carried her to our room, laid her back, and put the covers over her, before kissing her on the forehead. After she was in place, I fell to my knees and broke down.

The weight of the world was getting the better of me. I was trying so hard to make sure that everybody else was okay that it was killing me, and I was forgetting about myself. I felt myself getting dizzy. My heart started to beat really fast in my chest. I couldn't even breathe, though I was taking one deep breath after the next. I was thankful that Purity was asleep right then because I was sure that seeing me in that state would have freaked her out. I put my hand on my chest and felt my heart pounding at full speed. I sat on my ass and scooted all the way back to the wall, trying to get a hold of myself. My vision was blurry, and I felt like I was about to throw up. I slid down to my side and closed my eyes, still holding my chest. I didn't know how I was going to compensate everybody. I just knew that I had to, and that I would eventually figure it out, or it was going to kill me.

Chapter 9

The next day, Nikki woke me up earlier in the morning, around seven or so. She was knocking on my window, damn near about to climb through it. I say that because when I sat up in the bed, she had half of her head inside of my bedroom.

"Shemar, get yo' ass up, nigga, and meet me out front. I need to holla at you, and you ain't been answering yo' phone, once again." She rolled her eyes and jumped down from the windowsill. "Hurry up!"

Purity sat up in the bed with sleep all in her eyes. Her hair was all over the place and she looked worried. I tried to get out of the bed, but she wrapped her arms around my neck, pulling me down on to it. "No. No. No. Shemar, why you gotta go out there with her? Every time y'all leave together, you don't come back here until really late at night. I be worried out of my mind over you."

I unloosened her arms from around my neck and stood up. "I gotta go out here and get this money. You already know I gotta make it happen, so chill out, lil' sis." I slid into my boxers. I don't even remember how I'd gotten into the bed the night before. The last thing I remembered was laying on my side and struggling to breathe, but somehow I'd managed to.

Purity got out of the bed, naked, with panic written all across her face. She looked like she was about to have a nervous breakdown, and I was too because I kept imagining Nikki coming back to the window and seeing my sister standing in my bedroom, naked as hell. I didn't know what that would make her think of me.

"Shemar, can I got with you, then? Please? I don't wanna be in this house all day long with them hoes. I wanna be under you. I need you. Didn't I just tell you that last night?" She walked up to me and put both of her hands on my chest. "Please, can I come?"

I took a step back and slid up my Robin jeans, then put my wife beater over my head, tucking it into my pants before adding an all-black tee. I shook my head. "N'all, Purity, we on somethin'. Shit might get too dangerous, and I ain't finna have you out there in these streets with me like that. But I'll tell you what. I'll be back home early enough for me and you to go out to have dinner together since we ain't had a chance to do nothin' like that ever since you been stayin' here. I owe you some quality time. We'll do that tonight. Okay, sis?" I held out my arms for her.

She slowly walked into them with her bottom lip poked out, stomping her feet lightly. After she hugged me, she looked up. "Do you promise me that we'll go out tonight? Just me and you and nobody else?"

"I promise, it'll just be us; wherever you wanna go." I kissed her forehead.

As I was letting her go, prepared to throw my shoes on, Nikki jumped up to the windowsill, I guessed getting ready to tell me to come on. Just then, my bedroom door opened and Simone came into the room. When she saw Purity standing there naked, hugging me, her eyes got so big that I was surprised they didn't pop out of her head.

She looked Purity up and down, then shook her head. "I knew it." She slammed the door, and a few moments later, I could hear her slamming her own bedroom door.

Nikki's eyes were just as bucked. It looked like she was checking Purity out a lil' bit because her eyes were going up and down my sister's body, and then they stayed pinned on her gap. She sucked her bottom lip and made a noise deep within her throat.

Purity ran and jumped under the covers, throwing her head under them. "Remember what you promised me, Shemar. I'll be ready, too."

When I came out of the house, I saw that there was an all pink 2019 Lexus parked in front, with Nikki sitting behind the steering wheel, bobbing her head to the music coming out of the speakers. When I opened the passenger's door, I could hear the sounds of Cardi B spitting over the track. I knew that she was Nikki's second favorite rapper, behind Nicki Minaj. I slid into the seat, reached and turned down the music. "Who shit is this?"

She smiled. "This my shit. That nigga Taurus bought this bitch for me yesterday. He say he apologize for them niggas hitting me up, and this is my gift for inhaling them bullets and being so stomp down to you. He gave me this, too." She reached between her legs and pulled out a purple Crown Royal bag, dug her hand inside of it, and came up with a big bundle of hundred dollar bills. It had to be every bit of ten gees. "Nigga, how you love that?"

I took the money and thumbed through it, nodding, while she pulled away from the house. "You mean to tell me that he just gave you this shit? You ain't have to give him no pussy or nothin'?

She shook her head. "N'all, I didn't, but you know what? If he would have asked for some, I would have fucked him in the middle of the Lexus lot with no hesitation. Not only do he got stupid bread, but he fine as hell. He can definitely get this pussy. Shemar, you already know that this shit between my legs come at a price, and he more than paid for that. But speaking of pussy, what's up with you and Purity? Why was she hugging you all naked and shit? Y'all creepin' or somethin'?" She looked over to me before turning her eyes back on the road.

I exhaled. "N'all, we ain't did shit, but she want me to lay her down and make love to her. She talkin' 'bout that's the only way she can prove her love to me is if we fuck. Them Robinsons done fucked her head up."

Nikki shrugged. "She only yo' half-sister. If she want some dick, why don't you just give it to her? Shit, you fucking them other hoes in that house. She probably just jealous. What? You gon' let another nigga out here fuck on her or somethin'?"

As soon as I imagined that shit, I got ready to snap. I didn't want nobody touching Purity. I would kill a muhfucka quick if I found out anything like that. At the same time, I wasn't willing to cross them lines with her either, because no matter if she was just my half-sister or not, she was still my blood. I didn't believe in that half shit no way. She was my sister, bottom line. "Nikki, on some real shit, if I catch any nigga sniffing around my lil' sister, I'm bodying they ass on sight. Far as why I won't lay her down, is because that ain't right. She just hurtin' right now, and she feel like she gotta compete with the other females in the house, but that ain't the case. I'ma take her out tonight and spend some time with her— try and get her mind right, that's all."

Nikki smiled. "Shemar, yo' lil' sister fine as hell now. I didn't even know she was that thick either, but damn. I ain't gon' even lie, I was so used to looking at her like she was a kid, but after seeing all of that, I saw her through new eyes. Nigga, if I had yo' dick, I would lay her down. I'm just being honest. I couldn't stay away from that; half or whole." She flipped a switch and dropped the top to her whip.

I frowned. "Nikki, if you wasn't my right hand, and a female, I promise you I would knock yo' head off right for all of that shit you just said. You just don't understand how much I love Purity." I sat back in my seat as the hot sun beamed down on my forehead.

It was a lil' humid out already, and my stomach started to growl as well. I didn't really want to think about things from Nikki's angle because I felt like she was trying to poison my mind. My sister was just craving my affection, and she thought that the only way to prove that I would never leave her was if I laid her down, and that wasn't the case. I would try my best to show her that.

Nikki shrugged. "Just don't come to me for advice then, Shemar, because you know I'm gon' keep that shit one hundred. If I had yo' dick, and I had a sister that thick and fine walking around naked, all over me, I would tear that ass up, and wouldn't give a fuck what nobody say about it. Point-blank. But let's move on. I gotta take you to Buck City where we gotta meet up with Taurus. I guess he supposed to be putting you up on game about the first nigga you gotta handle. He didn't tell me much, only that I was gon' play a role."

I nodded. "Let's go, then. First, I need you to pull up to this McDonald's so I can put some food on my stomach."

She laughed. "What? You tired from running away from that ass all night?" After saying that, she bussed out laughing while I mugged her ass.

An hour later, we were pulling up in Buck City. We met up with Taurus outside of a strip club that he owned called Ms. Boujee. The club was known for having some of the best and baddest strippers in the game of all races. I mean, these females were super bad, strapped, and all about their paper. I was wishing that we had our lil' meeting inside of it just so I could catch a few glances of the talent there. Instead of going inside, we met up with him inside of a stretch Lincoln Navigator.

I followed Nikki to the back of the truck where she knocked on the glass. The next thing I knew, the front door opened. An old man with two tear drops on the left side of his face stepped out and opened the back door for us. "The boss is waiting for you two."

I let Nikki get in first, and then I climbed in behind her. The first thing I saw was that the interior was all Gucci, and the seats were leather. There was a big 4K television playing where the partition should have been, and on the screen was a bunch of stock information.

Taurus sat in the backseat with his ear glued to the phone, I imagined talking business. When he saw me, he smiled. "Shemar, I'll be right with you in a minute." He pointed to a small Gucci refrigerator. "Have some champagne."

Nikki laughed. "Shit, don't mind if I do." She opened the refrigerator, pulled out a bottle of Rosè, popped the cork, and handed me a champagne glass before filling it to the top. Afterward, she would drink out of the bottle. "Now, this is living."

I couldn't do nothing but laugh at her ghetto ass. It was the reason I loved her so much. It was because she was uncut and thorough.

Taurus hung up his phone about ten minutes later and exhaled loudly. "Awright, what it do, lil' homie?" He grabbed my hand and pulled me to him, giving me a half-hug before we broke apart.

"I'm good, bruh. Why you call me all the way out here to Buck City? I wish we would have had this meeting inside, that's for damn sure." I joked, but was more serious than anything. I wanted to see them broads.

He pointed at me with an index finger and smiled. "Nigga, you's a goon. You fucked that nigga Mickey over, and I loved how you did it. I'ma fuck with you the long way." He grabbed the bottle of Rosè from Nikki and turned it up. I watched his Adam's apple move up and down before he finished and handed her back the bottle.

She was so brazen that she licked all around the rim of it, sucking like a porn star while looking him in the eyes. "Yeah, Taurus, that's how I feel." She sucked the rim into her mouth and licked it all over again.

He shook his head. "This lil' girl gon' make me cheat on my wife, and I ain't never got down like that since we been together. But I can't lie, Nikki, you making it hard for me." He watched her cross her thick thighs. Her Fendi skirt was rising to her waist.

"Shit, first time for everything. My shit real tight 'cause I don't even fuck with niggas like that. When you ready, I'm giving you the green light." She opened her thighs wide, exposing her purple Victoria Secret laced panties. Then, she pulled them all the way up until her pussy mound was molded by the fabric.

Even I bucked my eyes out. I ain't know my right hand was holding like that. I closed her legs because I felt my dick getting super hard. "All that shit can wait, Nikki. We on business right now." She frowned, and I turned my attention to Taurus. "So, what's on yo' mind, boss man?"

He was gripping his piece. He reached into his Gucci pants and adjusted himself, shaking his head. "She gon' get me in trouble; I see that. But anyway, the reason why I called you out here is because I wanted to let you know that I approved of yo' work, and that it's time for you to go at these next two so I can put you on for the long haul. I want you to make two more statements to the game for me, and then you'll have your nod to enter Cloverland on your own right." He reached on the side of him and picked up the briefcase that had been sitting there. I had paid no attention to it until that moment. He opened it and came out of it with a picture. "Here. This is a nigga named Flyy. He got a lil' army of killas that rotate on the Westside of Cloverland, in Randolph row houses. He was second in line for Sherm's slot. If his slot is what you aiming for, you gon' have to knock him off, and then this nigga." He handed me another picture, and I curled my lip as soon as I saw the profile. "This is the first nigga that's in line for his slot. His name—"

"Vito," I said, cutting him off. "Yeah, I'm familiar with this cat, and I already had him on my radar more sooner than later, anyway, for some fuck shit he did a lil' while back against me and my right hand, sitting over there." I handed her the picture.

She scoffed. "When the time comes, I wanna be the one to body this nigga. Y'all gotta let me have that. I hate his bitch ass. Real talk."

"It's however y'all wanna do that shit," Taurus said, drinking from the bottle of champagne again. I noted he licked around the rim like Nikki had. They made eye contact, and I knew that they would be fuckin' one day soon. "Flyy gotta go by the morning, though. I'm tired of this nigga, and I could easily have him whacked, but then I would stand in the way of how this game goes, in regards to you stepping up on that throne, Shemar. You gotta kill in three's. Mickey was one, Flyy will be two, and you end the trinity with Vito. That's just how this shit go. It's the only way you'll get the key to the streets." He took another sip from the bottle, picked up a remote and turned the television to Sport's Center. "I gotta get them Cleveland scores from last night. I know LeBron did his thing. That's my nigga."

I was too busy mugging the picture of Flyy. I'd seen him around Cloverland on more than one occasion, always driving a foreign whip with an entourage of niggas behind him. He was famous for rocking all kinds of army fatigue outfits, and having big charms of four leaf clovers that were draped in green diamonds. A real flashy nigga.

I held the picture up to Taurus. "When is the best time to dispose of this nigga?"

Taurus grabbed Nikki's arm and made her sit on his lap. "You see, that's where she come in." He kissed her neck, then sucked on it, and opened her legs wide. His hand slipped up under her skirt, and I watched his fingers slip into the side of her panties before he was rubbing her bald brown pussy.

They were sitting directly across from me, giving me a crazy view. I ain't even gon' lie. I was hard as hell. I could smell a slight trace of Nikki's pussy in the air and it was intoxicating. I just loved the smell of pussy, period. Nikki laid her head back, and moaned into his neck while he played with her down low.

"You see, Shemar, Flyy thinks that just because Sherm is out of the game that he gon' automatically move upward, and I gave him the nod that he would be doing so. However, what he don't know is that I'm aware that he been skimming off of the top from the profits coming from the Westside of my operations in Cloverland. That shit alone is punishable by death. Why not kill two birds with one stone?"

"Unnn-a!" Nikki closed her eyes as Taurus' fingers moved in and out of her fat pussy. Her thick thighs were open so wide that it looked like she was giving birth to his wrist. Her panties were pulled all the way to the right side. The faster he fingered her, the heavier her scent blessed the air, making me feel some type of way. "Unn! Unn! Unn-a! Mmm-uh! Shit, daddy!"

"Whenever somebody moves up in my mob, Shemar, I bless them with a top-notch stripper for the night, who gets paid to make their dreams come true for four hours straight. That's what Flyy thinkin' he gone get tonight. He already laid up in a penthouse suite, and is expecting to have a girl with him tonight from one in the morning until five. That's where Nikki gon' come in. She gon' be the girl, and you gon' make a crazy statement to the game for me. I want his balls cut off and brought to me. It's time that I show these niggas how I really get down." He bit into Nikki's neck and started to finger her so fast that she had to put her hands on his shoulders, and a foot on the seat.

"Huh! Huh! Huh! Huh! Oh shit! Taurus! Taurus! Taurus! Shiiiitt!" Her hips started to buck into him over and over again, then she got to shaking real bad while his fingers went in and out of her. As soon as she finished cumming, she dropped to her knees and tried to get his dick out while he sucked her juices off of his fingers.

The way she was bent all the way over, she was exposing her pussy to me from the back. The lips were engorged and oozing her creams. I was aching by this point. I had never really looked at her in that light before, but I was finding it real hard not to. She was exposing so much, and it had been a few days since I had actually got me some.

He pushed her hands away and laughed. "N'all, shawty, we ain't gon' get down like that. I can't fuck over my wife, but I'm gon' sho' nuff let her know about you, and we gon' wind up laying you down together. Y'all are a lot alike. She'll be down for it. Trust me."

Nikki groaned as if she were in pain. "Taurus, fuck that. I need some of that dick, right now. You got me aching like a muhfucka." She tried to reach for his belt again, but he grabbed both of her wrists.

"N'all, shawty. With me, it's loyalty to my bloodline first. Let me holler at Princess. Once she gives me the go ahead, we gon' do this shit right. I promise." He helped her to come to a sitting position beside him, and she sat there, pouting like a big ass kid. He looked over at me. "Like I was saying. I'ma kill two birds with one stone. You saved my daughter's life, plus I like how you get down. So, I want you to have a slot in Cloverland. One where you eating like it's a buffet. In order to get that, you gotta knock these niggas out of the way, and I need them gone so I can start a new movement in these slums of Cloverland. One hand washes the other. I want this nigga's balls in front of me by nine in the morning. Get it done."

Chapter 10

It was five o'clock in the evening when I picked up Purity So we could go out and have our dinner together. She'd chosen a lil' Italian joint on the north side of town that specialized in lasagna that we both loved. The restaurant was nicely dimmed and had Frank Sinatra singing out of the speakers. On the low, I liked Frank Sinatra and all them old cuts. I felt like that music was soothing and it catered to that gangsta in me.

After we ordered our food, and snacked on a few bread sticks, Purity slid all the way around the booth until she was able to rest her head on my shoulder. Once she did that, she sighed out loud. "This is nice, Shemar. I wish that me and you could stay like this forever, and I never had to share you with nobody. You'd be all mine and I'd be the happiest girl in the world, with no worries." She looked up and kissed my neck, before laying her head back down on my shoulder.

The restaurant was kind of packed and a little noisy, with couples talking amongst themselves, mostly white people, but there were a few Spanish people there as well. I knew that me and Purity were the only blacks that I saw. It smelled good as hell in there. My stomach was growling like crazy.

I didn't even know it was making that much noise until Purity put her hand over my abs and rubbed them lower than she should have. "Dang, big bruh, you hungry, huh?" She laughed.

I put my arm around her and held her for a minute or two without saying a word. Kissing her on the top of the head, I noticed her smiling. "Sis, you know I love you more than anything or anybody in this world, right? You know I'll do anything for you, or over you, any day, right?"

She picked her head up and looked into my face as if she were worried about something. "Yeah, I know that. But why are you telling me this right now, Shemar? You're scaring me?" She whimpered, looking into my eyes.

I shook my head. "Ain't no reason for you to be scared. I'm just stating facts." I leaned down and put my forehead up against hers before giving her a peck on the tip of her nose. It was something that I used to do when we were little kids.

She smiled. "I know you'll do anything for me, Shemar. I never doubt that part of you. I just fear that one day Simone or her mom is going to take you away from me because they can give you some things that you won't take from me." She shook her head. "I can't take how I feel about you. I don't know why I feel like I feel, but I just can't help it. I know I'm not the first girl to have a crush on her brother, and I damn sure won't be the last. Do you hate me because of how I feel? Am I weird to you?" She continued to rub my stomach.

Her hand had gotten lower to the point that her pinky and ring fingers were under my boxer's band, rubbing along my hairs inside of them. I guessed because I didn't say anything she thought it would be okay to sneak her hand all the way down inside of them. She grabbed hold of my piece, squeezing it, then holding it in her hand.

I ain't gon' even lie and say that I wasn't hard as hell because I was. I wasn't thinking clearly. After seeing all of that shit with Nikki and Taurus, and Purity steady coming at me, mixed with the fact that I hadn't gotten no pussy in a few days, the feel of her stroking my pipe was doing it for me. Being in that restaurant helped too. It made it that much more taboo.

I closed my eyes as she unbuttoned my jeans and unzipped them. Then, she pulled my piece through my boxer's hole and breathed on the head. An image of Nikki's fat pussy came into my mind. I saw the thick sex lips, her juices, and the look on her face as Taurus was fingering her. All of that shit was driving me crazy.

"N'all, lil' sis, you ain't weird to me. It's okay to feel how you feel. We just can't do nothin' about it because we family. Mmm-shit."

She sucked me into her mouth and licked my head as if it was an ice cream cone. Then, she swallowed me whole and started to suck loudly, moaning all around him. My eyes rolled into the back of my head. I was thankful that the place was so dark. I saw images of Purity's naked frame in my mind— her thighs and the way her cat sat in between them. Then I saw Nikki on all fours, bussed open. I imagined the both of them playing around like I'd had Simone and her mother before. That shit was so hot to me.

The heat of her mouth was causing my toes to curl. I reached over her shoulder and cupped her big ass, soft booty. As I was squeezing it, I pulled her skirt up to expose the red thong that separated her yellow ass cheeks. I had brought her there to get an understanding, and to let her know that we could never cross that line, but I had lost all of my will power. Everything that Nikki had said was getting the better of me.

Purity sucked me faster and faster. I opened my eyes to see her titties bouncing into one another. The sight of them caused me to get even more riled up. I started humping into her mouth and I was so embarrassed. I knew better. I knew I wasn't supposed to be doing that shit. I was bogus. I hated myself.

When she pulled me out of her mouth, she licked the head and rubbed it all over her face before deep throating me all over again. It was all I could take. I felt my seed rising in my sack. My abs tightened, and then I was letting it fly all into her mouth.

"Mmmm. Mmmm. Mmmm," was all she said as she milked me with her eyes closed and had a big smile on her face. It was the first time that I also noticed that she had her hand between her legs inside of her panties, going to town.

I jumped out of my skin when I located the waiter coming over with our food. I pulled her up and pointed. Her eyes got big while she pulled her skirt down and sat back in the booth. I couldn't even make eye contact with her as we ate our food. I was feeling so guilty. I didn't have no self-control, and I knew that would be my downfall one day.

Purity looked across the table and lowered her head. "Shemar, it's okay. We love each other. Don't make it seem like we just did somethin' wrong. I need you in that way. I need to know that I can satisfy you in that way, just like any other female can. You said you'd do anything for me. Well, I need your body from time to time until I can get my head back right, to be strong enough to mess with an outside dude."

I shook my head. "You my sister, Purity. Damn. I wasn't supposed to let that shit happen. You just keep coming and coming, though, and we been away from each other for so long that I find myself peeping you in a way that I shouldn't be. You too damn bad, that's the problem. That and I ain't got no fuckin self-control."

She smiled. "Well, when it comes to me, I don't want you to have none. I want you to make love to me, Shemar in the real way. I wanna feel what they feel. We ain't gotta do it all the time, but I need to feel it at least once. Every boy that ever got on top of me, I hated. So, I don't know what it feels like to have somebody make love to me that actually cares about me, and I care about them. I hate myself everyday when I look in the mirror because of that fact. Only you can heal that ugliness in me." She looked into my eyes and smiled weakly. "I need you so freaking bad."

My head was spinning as I sat there, looking into her eyes. I saw all of the hurt and pain that she strug-gled to mask on a daily basis. I saw a woman in need of love and protection. She needed to be validated. She needed to be treasured, and I guess I was the only one that she could turn to with all of those issues.

We sat there for a long time, just looking at each other. I had so many things going through my head all at once that I felt my brain trying to shut down. I saw Purity's mouth moving, but I couldn't compre-hend what was coming out of it. I was too far gone.

I don't know how it happened or how we got there, or I probably do, but somehow, my mind was trying to slowly erase the truth. But somehow, we wound up at the Hyatt Regency Hotel and I had it in my mind that I was going to give Purity everything that she needed. That, for this night, I just wasn't going to think.

It was going to be all about healing her by any and every means. It was all that would matter. But after the door closed behind us, I still couldn't bring myself to move toward her in a sexual manner because what I saw was my lil' sister. No matter how hard I tried to will myself to give her what she wanted, I just couldn't bring myself to make the first move.

I stood with my back to the door of the hotel room while Purity sat on the bed for a second, looking over at me.

Then, she took her Red Bottoms off, stood, pulled her Gucci skirt over her head, and slowly walked over to me until she was standing in my face so close that I could smell her perfume. "Shemar, all you gotta do is look at my body. You'll see that I ain't no lil' girl no more. I'm a woman, and I need you down here." She took my hand and rubbed it up against the front of her panties as she spread her thighs to make sure that I got a good feel of her monkey. She pressed my fingers into her sex lips, while she sucked on her bottom lip and moaned deep within her throat.

Her cat felt puffy. The lips were thick and I could see their indentation through her panties. The longer she used my finger to rub up and down her crease, the wetter she got, and the further her panties went inside of her lips.

"Mmm-a, Shemar, let's just do this and get it over with." She closed her eyes and stepped forward, biting me on the neck and unbuckling my Ferragamo belt, before unbuttoning my pants and pulling them down, along with my boxers.

My dick sprung up like a brown cucumber, hard and ready to go. All it took was for her to wrap her little hand around it and I lost it. I decided right then that I was gon' do it, and like she said, get it over with. We never had to do it again if things didn't go right. I just wanted to be there for her and to help her get whatever it was that she had in her system out of her. So, as her little hand was pumping my dick, and she looked like she was about to drop to her knees to give me some more like she had done in the restaurant, I pulled her up by her arm then scooped her in the air, making her wrap her thick thighs around me, before sucking all over her lips.

"Mmm-yes. Shemar. Yes, big bruh, it's my turn now. It's my turn, big bruh. It's my turn for you to show me the love that you been showing them. Please." She moaned and started kissing me back, and sucking all over my lips loudly.

I carried her by her ass to the bed, and laid her back, getting between her thighs, kneeling and opening her legs wider. I sucked on the crotch band of her panties, and licked up and down her crease, then pulled her panties to the side, exposing her fat sex lips. Then, I leaned forward and sucked them into my mouth. Afterward, I took my tongue and licked all up and down her center, while her juices dripped off of my chin.

She humped into my face, grabbing my head. "Unn. Unnn. Shit, Shemar. Eat me, baby. Eat lil' sis. Uhhhh! Yes! I love you so much!" She moaned, but I was in my own zone.

I peeled apart her lips and sucked on her clit, hard. With my tongue, I pushed it as far into her as it would go.

She gripped my head harder and humped up off of the bed in a frenzy. "Hmm-a. Hmm-a. I can't. I can't take it. Shemar! Shemar! Shemar! Uhhhhhh! Sheeiitttt!" Her hips started to work overtime while her thighs clamped around on my head.

I kept on eating, slurping and licking, going for what I knew.

She sat all the way up, then fell on her back to the bed, and came screaming loudly, "Ahhhhhh! Shemarrrr!" Her pussy squirted into my face, and I kept on eating, attacking her clit and swallowing her juices.

After she finished shaking, she pulled me on top of her, wrapped her arms around my neck, sucking all over my lips. She was tasting her own pussy juices, I imagined. It all turned me on even more. I was in my own zone. I was seeing Nikki. I was seeing Simone, and even my foster mother. I reached between us and pulled her panties all the way down and off, then slid out of my boxers.

I took my dick head and rubbed it up and down her crease while she moaned deep within her throat. "Tell me, Purity. Tell me that this is what you really want, sis. Tell me that you need me in this way, and

I'm gon' give you all that you need from me. But you gotta tell me this." I felt her heat scorch my dick's head.

Her nipples stood at attention, hard. There was a puddle forming between our middles. She moaned, "I need you so bad, Shemar. I need you so, so bad. I want you to put it in me and treat me like yo' girl. I want you to make love to me. I need it so, so bad. Please-a." She reached between us and moved my hand out of the way. Opening her thick thighs real wide, she slowly guided me into her while she bit on her bottom lip. "Unnnn. Mmmm-a. I feel you, big bruh. It feels so good. Now keep telling me how much you love me while you do it to me. Unnn. Tell me you love me the most. Unnn. Shit. Tell me that you love me more than anybody else, and heal me." She moaned with tears rolling down her cheeks.

I was just praying that they were happy tears because the lines had been crossed, and there was no turning back. I didn't know if I was doing the right thing. All I cared about was giving my sister what she needed. I would have given her my life if it would have made her happy. She was my everything, and there was nothing that I wouldn't do for her. I slid all the way into her box, and hit bottom. Her lips sucked at me, and her walls tried to squeeze me to death. She felt hot and super wet. As much as I hate to admit it, her lil' cat was fire.

I got to sliding in and out of it with a nice rhythm. "I love you, Purity. I love you so much, baby." I put her thighs on my shoulders and kept on going. "Umm. Umm. Huh. Mmm. Shit. I love you, lil' sis. I'll do anything for you. Any. Thing. You. Hear.

Me?" Back and forth, harder and harder, I sped up the pace.

Her juices were oozing out of her. She closed her eyes, and I could see the look of euphoria on her face. "Yes. Yes. Keep fucking me, Shemar. Keep fucking me, Shemar. Mmmm. I love you, Shemar. I'm yours. I'm yours. Uhhhh-shit! Uhhhh! I'm yoo-ouuuurrrrsssss!" She reached around my waist and dug her nails into me while she came again and again.

I sped up the pace and really started to kill that pussy like I was supposed to— going as deep as I possibly could. Her walls felt like they were trying to suck me further into her body. I got to going super-fast. *Bam. Bam. Bam. Bam. Bam. Bam. Bam.* Harder and harder, pushing her knees further to her shoulders, I let her have it. If we were gon' get it in, I might as well let her know how I really got down in that bedroom, even though I wanted to spare her a lil bit. She wasn't going for that.

"Harder, Shemar. Oooh. You in my stomach. Harder, baby. Fuck me as hard as you can. Don't play with me. I love you so much. Uhhh!"

I got to digging deep within her, then faster and faster. The bed was going haywire. I mean that mu-hfucka was beating against the wall like it was trying to go through, and that pussy was feeling so good that I couldn't stop. I leaned down and sucked on her neck, then her tittes. The nipples were standing up a cool inch.

When I felt her cum, and she was shaking against me, it caused me to splash my seed into her. "Huh.

Huh. Huh. Uhhhh-shiiit!" My abs started jerking and I came deep with her.

She screamed at the top of her lungs. "Yes! Yes! Yessssss!"

I wasn't ready to call it a day yet. Though, as soon as I released within her, I got up and flipped her onto her stomach, biting into the back of her neck while I pushed her right knee to her ribs, and entered her again, long-stroking her slowly. "I love you, Purity. I belong to you first. You're my everything. I will always be there for you, first and foremost. Do you understand me? Huh?" I grabbed her tittie from the side and squeezed it.

She bounced her ass back into my lap, again and again, taking all of my dick, milking me and leaving me all greasy at my center. It seemed like the deeper I stroked her, the wetter she got. The way she slammed her ass into my lap was driving me crazy. In my opinion, there was nothing like a big ass booty smashing into you.

"Yes. Yes, Shemar. I understand. This is all that I wanted. This is it. I just wanted you inside of me. It feels so good. I love you do much. Just keep telling me that you love me first. Just me, while you dick me down to sleep. Please." She moaned and slammed back harder into my lap. The sounds of her pussy was heard as clear as day now. I sped up the pace and got to killing it once again. "Uhhhh! Mmmm! You fuckin' me so hard! You fuckin' me so harddddddd! Ahhhh!" She screamed and came all over me again.

I kept on pounding with all of my might. It got to feeling too good, and the next thing I knew, I was letting loose deep within her again. This time I fell on that big ass booty and kept right on pumping for the next hour, slowly, while we came all over each other. I held her close with me telling her how special she was to me, and how much I loved her more than everybody else. Before it was all said and done, me and Purity stayed up for most of that night, getting an understanding. As crazy as it may sound, after we got that understanding, I didn't feel guilty about what we did. I mean, I didn't know if we would ever do it again, but what I did know was that I would be there for her in any way that she needed me and whenever she needed me. I didn't give a fuck about what the world thought about it, and I still don't.

Chapter 11

That same night, after I took Purity home and tucked her in the bed, I met up with Nut two blocks over from my crib. I was in good spirits and ready to body that nigga Flyy so I could work on getting plugged in with Taurus. I had to get my weight all the way up so I could take care of Purity and get us financially stable in the world. I knew we couldn't bank on staying with my mother forever, even though she wanted us to. I just felt that sooner or later, me fucking all three females in the house would catch up with me, and I was gon' have to choose one of them and stick with it. The one I chose was gon' have to go through hell, and I ain't want that because I was gon' choose Purity every time. So, I needed to get right, and the first step to doing that was killing Flyy.

It was about four in the morning when I jumped in his whip with a smile on my face. I didn't know why I was smiling. I guessed because I was feeling good, but it seemed like it annoyed him.

"Sun, why you got that dumb ass smile on yo' face, Kid. It's too early in the morning." He looked me over closely with a mug on his face, then pulled away from the curb.

I waved him off. "Fuck what you talking about. I'm in a good mood. I had a bunch of shit that was weighing me down, but now it ain't. I'm good and I'm ready to handle this business." I sat back in my seat and tried to vibe out to the homie Yo Gotti as he spat through the speakers.

Nut laughed. "Yeah, well, nigga, you smell like pussy. So, that explains that dumb ass look. Far as this body goes, let's handle this shit so I can get back to sleep. Word is bond. I been fuckin' all night too, and shorty laid back up at the room with two pills in her, waiting for the god to get back." He extended his fist and we dapped while laughing and shit.

About thirty minutes later, we were sneaking through the fire escape that Nikki had left open for us at the Hotel. I looked both ways before stepping inside of the carpeted hallway. Once I saw that the coast was clear, I stepped into it, followed by Nut, and we took the hallway until we got to the presidential suite. Once there, I slid down my mask and watched Nut do the same. The key card, just as Nikki had promised, was at the bottom of the door, slid half way under it. In order for a person to have peeped it, they would've had to be looking for it, which I was. I kneeled and picked it up, took a deep breath and slid it into the slot. The door's face flicked from red to green, then the door popped open.

As soon as it did, I could hear the sounds of SZA coming out of the speakers. The lights were low, and I heard crystal glasses clinking together.

I stepped all the way in, and from my vantage point, I could see Nikki off in the distance slow grinding on Flyy's lap, giving him a sensual lap dance with her head tilted backward. Her hips rotated in a circular motion. She didn't have a bra on, so her titties jiggled while she did her thing. I never knew that she could get down like that. I watched Flyy's hands paw at her thick, caramel thighs. She spread them, and his other hand dipped into her middle.

"Damn, baby girl, I ain't seen a bitch as fine as you in a long time. I'ma wind up giving you all ten of these gees, and that includes me giving you a tip for fucking this pussy. You got my nose open and shit." He leaned over and tooted up a line of cocaine.

Nikki continued to ride him with her back arched and both hands on her knees. "Ummm. I'm just giving you what you deserve, boss. Taurus told me to treat you like a king, so that's what I'm doing." She licked her lips and closed her eyes.

I wasn't with that shit. I stepped out of the shadows with Nut behind me. "Well, Taurus told me to treat you like a bitch, so that's what I'ma do." I had the .45 pointed at him sideways. I wanted to blow that nigga head off after seeing my right hand man grinding all on him and shit. I had to admit that I was a lil' jealous. That shit pissed me off.

Flyy's eyes bugged out of his head, then he threw his hands in the air. "Man, what the fuck is this? I work for Taurus."

"Nikki, get the fuck off this nigga and put some clothes on." I snapped way harder than I meant to. I knew that she was doing her job, but I still didn't like that shit. Dude had his hands all over her thighs. It made me feel sick on the stomach.

Nikki got off of him and punched him straight in the mouth. *Wham!* His head jerked backward and he fell half way out of the chair. "Bitch nigga, that's for every time that you called me a bitch! Respect me as being a woman, not a bitch." She punched him again and backed up.

This time, he fell off of the chair, onto his side. He looked like he was reaching under the bed and feeling around for something, but Nut was on his ass.

He ran over there at full speed and picked Flyy up into the air by his throat, choking the shit out of him. "What you reachin' for, Kid? Huh? Fuck you reaching fo', nigga?"

Flyy feet dangled in the air while Nikki dove under the bed and came up with an Uzi that had an extended clip. Had that nigga gotten his hands on that, we would've all been dead. Luckily Nut got the jump on him.

Nikki backed away with the Uzi and finished getting dressed. "Kill this nigga, Shemar. This nigga ain't got no loyalty whatsoever. All he kept on saying was that he finna be king of Cloverland. That everybody was gon' bow down to him. He say Taurus ain't even from Houston, so the streets don't owe him no honor."

"Is that right?" I asked, walking up to him, pulling the knife out of the small of my back while Nut held him in a full Nelson.

Flyy kicked his feet and tried to break free, but wasn't nothing happening. He only looked like he weighed about one seventy, and Nut was every bit of two sixty. He had him penned all the way up. His feet weren't even touching the ground.

Flyy shook his head. "Say, look, man. This ain't that. I got love for fam. I was just jacking fo' the bitch. You know how playas play." He looked from Nikki to me with a worried look on his face.

Nikki scrunched her face. "And you gon' call me a bitch again, after I just got done knocking yo' punk ass out the chair?" She frowned. "You know what, Shemar? Let me see that fuckin' knife. I'll handle this one."

With no hesitation, I gave it to her and stood back. I loved seeing her in action. I got to kill shit all the time, but whenever I got to tune into her doing it, it just made it that much more special. There was nothing more special than seeing a female kill a nigga. Especially if he was trifling like that nigga Flyy. Nut held him up and bear hugged his ass.

Nikki walked up on him, smiling. She licked her juicy lips, then curled her upper one. "Fuck niggas just don't learn." She stabbed forward and planted the blade in his stomach while he hollered.

"Awww! Shit! What the fuck you doing?" Blood poured out of him and around the blade that was still embedded deep within him.

Nikki pulled it out and slammed it back into him. This time she pulled it upward, slicing him open as if she were performing a strange version of a C-section. His guts slowly spilled out of him and dropped to the carpet, turning it burgundy. After all of that started to drop out of him, Nut let him go.

Flyy fell to his knees with blood pouring out of his midsection and mouth. He crawled around like a confused baby. I stood back with a smile on my face. I ain't know what that nigga was going through, but I was glad it was him and not me.

I tapped Nikki on the shoulder and made her give me the knife, reluctantly. Once in my hands, I watched him crawl around for a lil' while slowly bleeding out. Then, I stomped him in the back and made him fall to his stomach. Afterward, I sat on his back, stabbed him in the ass, right to the left side of his crack, and ripped the blade downward to create a hole in his boxers.

Once that was complete, I stuck my hand inside of the hole and grabbed a hand full of his nuts, before slowly sawing them off while he gasped in pain, choking on the blood coming out of his mouth and nose. When I turned around, Nikki was already holding the Ziploc bag for me to drop them into.

Afterwards, we would book it to Nikki's new apartment that Taurus had bought her, completely furnished. Nut plopped on the couch and laid his head on the arm rest before dosing off. I sent Taurus a message, letting him know that everything was taken care of and that he should get at me when it was confirmed.

Nikki changed clothes and waltzed into the living room, holding a box of Pizza Hut pizza, already chewing on a slice that was in her left hand. "I don't care what black folks be talking about. Them white people got cold pizza figured out. This shit taste way better than it did last night. Here." She handed me the box and I opened it up to reveal a Meat Lover's pizza with stuffed crust.

I sat that box on my lap, took a slice, and bit into it like I was starving. I actually felt like I was. I had put in some major work with Purity, and now I was starting to feel the hunger pains from it.

Nikki sat across from me in her little boy shorts that rode into her crack once she crossed her thick thighs. She took another bite from her pizza and smiled with her eyes closed. "Shemar, I'm surprised you ain't said nothin' about this crib that this nigga bought me. Usually you would have been snapped out. So, what's good?" She opened her eyes and looked over at me.

I had a mouthful of pizza, chewing it nice and slow, enjoying the taste of it. I definitely was about to get all in her ass about this nigga buying her this crib, but I had to get my energy up first. So, I kept on chewing with my eyes closed, not paying her no mind. I knew that would irritate her ass, and I was right.

She slammed her slice of pizza down on the lamp table and got up. "What? Because you fuckin' that bitch and her momma, I don't matter no moe or somethin'?" She put her hand on her hip, mugging the shit out of me.

"Damn, shut up, Nikki. You acting like you his bitch or somethin'. He ain't gotta be mad 'cause some nigga tricking his chips on you. That's how the game go. Now, let me sleep," Nut grumbled.

"Shut the fuck up, Nut! Damn! This ain't got shit to do with you. This between me and him." She rolled her eyes. "And why don't you go in the guest room if you wanna sleep, because I'm finna get to the bottom of this shit with him. So, bye."

Nut stood up and grabbed his pistol off of the couch, mugged Nikki, and then shook his head when walking past her. "Word is bond. Y'all must be fuckin' or somethin' 'cause you tripping more than a vacation right now." He continued on down the hall-way until I heard the door slam.

Then, Nikki turned her eyes back to me after mugging the back of his head as he walked to the room. "Well, Shemar, what gives? How you letting this nigga buy me shit and you ain't saying nothin' about it? What? You don't care about yo' right hand no more, since you fucking Simone and her momma?" She zoomed into my eyes with her own.

I threw my crust in the box and closed it, rubbing my hands together until she got the hint and handed me a bunch of napkins. Then, I stood up and shrugged. "What you want me to say, Nikki? Huh?"

She sucked her teeth. "I want you to say that you don't like hearing about no nigga buying me shit because you don't need him to. That the only man I need in my life is you, and that you ain't geeing for no nigga steppin' on yo' toes, whether me and you fuckin' or not, because it's always been that way. Say somethin', because, right now, I ain't feeling no type of love from you at all and it's fuckin with my brain. It's making me feel lost as a muthafucka. Ever since I got shot, you just been different. I don't understand what's going on with us. Do you still care or not?"

I exhaled loudly, and walked over to her in an attempt to hug her, but she took a step back.

"N'all, fuck all that hugging shit. Speak, nigga, and tell me what's good." She crossed her arms over her chest and tapped her pedicured toes on the white carpet.

I lowered my head, then looked back up at her. "You already know I don't like this shit. Ever since we been kids, I been the only nigga in yo' life that made shit happen for you when you needed it, or we did that shit together. Now, here come Taurus, tricking these chips off on you like it ain't nothin'. I gotta admit that I'ma lil' jealous, but I just feel like you got this shit under control. At least I hope you do. At the same time, I got so much shit on my plate that it's fuckin with my health." I went and sat back down on the couch because my vision was starting to go blurry.

Nikki came and squatted in front of me with her thighs wide open. I knew she wasn't on no sexual shit, but at the same time, them boy shorts went all up in her gap. I couldn't deny peepin' that shit because her lips popped out on each side of the panties. "What do you mean it's fuckin' with yo' health?" She looked worried and a lil' sick.

I closed my eyes and tried to gain my composure. "I been getting these crazy headaches and my vision be going blurry and shit. I think I'm stressing too much and it's fuckin with my blood pressure or somethin'. I don't know." I exhaled loudly.

She rubbed my back and got a lil' closer. "Is there somethin' that I can do for you? Just name it and you already know I'ma hold you down." She rubbed the side of my face, sucking on her bottom lip like she always did when she was nervous or worried about something important.

I flared my nostrils and exhaled again before putting my head down. "I fucked Purity last night, and that shit getting to me a lil' bit." I really didn't know if it was as much as I made it seem right then, but I just wanted to know what she was gon' say, or if she was gon' shame me or not.

She stood up and scrunched her face, looking me over for a long time. "What you mean you fucked her? You mean like put yo' dick in her pussy?"

I nodded, still keeping it lowered, but occasionally making eye contact with her. I guess since I didn't say nothing she figured that's exactly what I meant.

"Well, how do she feel about it? Did she cry afterwards, or did she want to do it again?" She came and sat next to me on the couch, grabbing my hand and interlocking her fingers with them.

I shrugged. "She liked that shit, and she say she want us to do it from time to time. But I don't know how to feel about it, because just being honest with you, I don't feel as guilty as I probably should. What you think?"

She raised her left eyebrow. "Honestly?"

I nodded. "You already know that's what I expect."

"Shemar, you fine as hell, and you got a rock-hard ass body. If you were my brother, I'd be fuckin' you every day on the low, and the world would never find out about it. I know plenty hoes that get down like that. Most of them bitches in that lil' lesbian circle I be fuckin' with get down like that. They just don't want nobody to know it. I honestly don't feel like y'all did nothin' wrong because you love that girl, and she need you. Just don't get her pregnant or nothin', 'cause even though y'all only halves, that baby might still have some problems." She leaned over and kissed my cheek. "You good, nigga. How was it? And keep it real, too?" She looked me over closely.

I smiled and shook my head. At first I wasn't gon' even go there with her, but I figured why not? I had already gone this far. I nodded my head. "It was straight. Let's just say she blessed just like me."

Nikki shook her head, and I noted she was rubbing her thighs together a lot. "N'all, fuck that, Shemar. I want details just like you be giving me when it comes to other females. Her lil' ass super thick, so I know it had to be the bomb. Dish that tea, nigga, fa real. Let me sit on yo' lap, too." She moved my hand out of the way, and planted her big booty right in the center of my lap, and grinded a little. "Now, tell me, and don't be shamed either. The thought of you and her getting down together is driving me crazy." She picked my hands up and put them on her thighs, making me rub them up and down with her hands on top of mine. "Mmm. Did you take it easy on her, or did you treat her ass like she was supposed to be treated? I know you love thick hoes, so you had to have fun. But that's Purity, though. Damn, that's hot." She moved from sitting on my lap to just sitting on my right leg, straddling it, opening her legs all the way and rubbing her pussy up and down my thigh with her eyes closed. "Before you tell me about that, Shemar, I want you to tell me that you still my protector. That I'm still yo' right hand, and you'll kill a nigga over me quick, just like I know you will. Tell me that I still matter, and that if this nigga Taurus get too close, that you'll body his ass over me." She rubbed her pussy into me harder.

I saw that the material was all up in her ass and it was starting to make me feel some type of way, even though she was my right hand man.

I was so thankful when the doorbell rang just a few seconds after she told me what she wanted to hear me say. She hopped up off of my lap with the majority of her ass cheeks exposed. The boy shorts cuffed her monkey from the back, and I was hard as hell. I wanted to fuck her this day. Bad.

She peeked out of the window, then smiled back at me. "It's Taurus. You got them balls ready for him, so we can get on to the next mission?"

Chapter 12

Taurus held up the Ziploc that held Flyy's balls inside of it and smiled. "This that real nigga shit, right here. That's why I'm finna help you eat, lil' nigga. You, and my baby right here." He wrapped his arms around Nikki while she stood in front of him with her ass backed into his crotch.

From the front, I could see her camel toe through her panties. I wanted to smoke that nigga Taurus for holding her like that.

"So, what's next, big homie? I'm ready to body this last nigga, so I can get the key to the streets. All you gotta say is when and how, and it's done." I trailed my eyes down and saw Nikki moving her ass all around on him while she looked me in the eyes.

If I wasn't tripping, I could swear that she was trying to make me jealous, and that shit was working. I was ready to lose my cool over her, and I didn't fully understand why. Maybe it was the fact that I had never seen her all over no dude other than me before. She mostly fucked with females, but ever since she had gotten out of the hospital, she had been all about dick, and I didn't like it. We had been friends our whole lives and had never gotten down before, but now I was seeing her in a different light. Her body was doing something to me that it never had before.

Taurus leaned down and kissed her behind the left ear. "Look, Shemar, before you handle this next nigga, I wanna take you somewhere with me and show you some shit. After I lace you with that part of the game, then we can move forward. That's cool with you?" He went into his pocket and pulled out a fat knot of hundreds, handing them to Nikki.

She took them, smiled, and turned around to flash her wedgie before tonguing him down while he rubbed all over her ass cheeks. He opened them and everything. I was getting heated and feeling like a straight sucka.

About three in the afternoon, that same day, I found myself sitting on a yacht with Taurus and some nigga with long dreads named Hood Rich. The nigga Hood Rich had so many colorful diamonds all over him that I kept thinking about robbing his ass, even before he introduced himself to me as he got on the boat.

"What's good, Jo? My name Hood Rich. You must be the lil' nigga that Taurus been telling me about." He extended his hand for me to shake, and I noticed the iced lemonade Rolex on his wrist. The sun was beaming super hard on it, causing it to twinkle in the light.

I shook his hand and nodded. "Yeah, I'm Shemar, and I'm trying to get down with the homie out in Cloverland. I heard yo' name ringing through the slums. You from Chicago, right? You that big wig that fuck with Meech and the Rebirth heroin?" I knew I sounded funny exposing all of that, but I just wanted to let him know that I was hip to who he was and that I kept my ear to the streets of the slums.

He smiled with a mouth full of diamonds that looked like colorful iced Skittles. Once again, the sun attacked his jewelry and made them twinkle and glisten in its rays. "Yeah, Jo, that's me. But I don't fuck with that nigga Meech like that no moe. That's another story for another day."

I scrunched my face. "I thought Meech was dead. Word in the slums is that he was cut into a hundred pieces after crossing you."

Taurus laughed and looked over to Hood Rich after slapping his hand on my shoulder. "Say, man, let's quit with all that hearsay. We ain't here to talk about that no way. We here to discuss how you finna flood Cloverland after you make that last move. Now, follow me inside of the cabin. I wanna show you something."

I noticed that Hood Rich had two big brief cases with him as he walked ahead of me and Taurus inside of the cabin. The Yacht swayed from side to side as we sailed out into the water. Up ahead I saw a caramel skinned strapped female with a pink, two-piece Burberry bikini on, steering the ship.

I damn near got caught up until Taurus stepped in front of me and leaned down into my face. "Shemar, always remember that loose lips get niggas murdered on sight. Now, all that shit you just said to Hood Rich could get you killed because its privileged information. Always keep yo' knowledge of the slums in here." He put his finger to my temple. "And never let a muthafucka know what you know. You use that shit to benefit you. Do you understand me, young souljah?"

I nodded. "That's my bad, big homie. I just wanted that nigga to know that I know who he is."

Taurus shook his head. "It's always better to play the fool than to play the one with all of the brains. The more you know, the quicker you die in this game. Silence is the first key to the streets." He looked over my shoulders and squinted. "Now go on inside and take a seat. Princess, what you doing, ma?" He walked off toward where I saw the female steering the Yacht.

When I got to the bottom of the cabin, Hood Rich was just putting the eighth kilo of dope on the table that was packaged with Abraham Lincoln's face on it. He looked up and smiled at me. "This that shit right here, lil' dawg. This the shit that's finna have you completely take over Cloverland. If my nigga Taurus vouching for you, then you one hundred, and we finna go hard. Just pay attention. Have a seat."

I sat down at the table as Taurus came through the door and laid his hand on my shoulder. "You remember that Rebirth shit that you was talking about earlier? Well, here it is, live and in living color. The homie Hood Rich about to help me help you bless the game with this shit. This should let you know right now that I'm serious about you stepping up on that throne, lil' homie."

I walked over to the table where Hood Rich was just opening the second briefcase.

Once opened, he picked up a kilo of the heroin and handed it to me. "You see this one brick, right here, is worth one hundred and fifty gees. This shit pure and ain't been stepped on one time."

Taurus smiled. "Every time them feens take a dose of this shit, they be willing to give they life for the next one. You gotta be completely careful with it though, because they'll kill you for this shit too. You can't be treating them like crackheads, because heroin addicts and crackheads are too different breeds of feens. With heroin addicts, they'll be more loyal to you, and will give you everything they got until it's all gone. They'll hustle like a muthafucka to make sure that they have what they need from you because their body grows physically dependent on the drug that you're pushing. If the dope is good and you're consistent, they will be as well because, unlike crack-heads, a heroin addict can't afford to play Russian Roulette with a bunch of different dealers. If they get the wrong batch, it could kill them. So, once they find out that yours is top notch, with you is where they will establish their loyalties. Crackheads are cut-throat, and can afford to burn as many bridges that are set before them. They are bottom feeders and can't be trusted as much as heroin addicts. But the only upside to crackheads is, if you deny them your dope, they won't think about killing you as often as a heroin addict will."

He took the kilo back from me. "This ain't no av-erage heroin here, though. It's been juiced up by the homie Hood Rich here, and cut with a nice amount of Fentanyl. He been doing this shit for a long time, and we were able to lace Memphis with his guidance, but that's another story. Bottom line, this is your in lil' homie. After you handle this last bit of business, I'ma get you set up in the building right where Flyy used to be, because they need new management over there, and that's where you come in. I got you though. Trust me."

Hood Rich smiled and closed the briefcases back after Taurus handed him back the last kilo of dope. "Lil' dawg, if you trust him, you'll be straight. I feed who my lil' nigga tell me to feed. Trust and believe, he earned his stripes, and he street certified with the higher ups. He got love for you, then the slums do too. You got my stamp of approval."

After that, Taurus sat me down for the next hour, explaining to me how potent the Rebirth really was. It said that he was putting me in an area where the feens lived and died by the drug. He told me to be careful because the drug could change my life for the better or for the worst. The more he talked, the more I tried to soak up. I wasn't trying to miss a beat. I wanted to eat in the slums and get full. I wanted to pick his brain as much as I possibly could, so I asked a lot of questions, and long after Hood Rich left, Taurus stayed back and answered every one of them until I had an understanding as to what I was getting myself into. His parting words is what stuck to me the most.

He pulled up in front of my crib and turned off his ignition. I was just about to get out of the car when he grabbed my arm. "Wait, Shemar. Listen to me, and listen carefully. When it comes to these streets and my money, I won't ever hesitate to take yo' life, and it'll never be personal; it's just how the game goes. I can't allow for you to cross me in no type of way. Nor can I allow for you to fuck up my operation. I'll give you one warning. After that, I gotta take yo' life, lil' homie. This shit ain't a game. I see a lot of me in you, and with that being said, I never wanted the niggas in the game to take it easy on me. I never wanted to be coddled. If I fucked up, I expected for my brains to be knocked out, and you gotta think the same way. That way, you won't make any mistakes. You feel me?"

I continued to look at the floor of his Jaguar and nodded. "Yeah, I do."

I didn't like for nobody to threaten my life, but I understood what he was saying. I wasn't looking for nobody to take it easy on me. I was about to go hard for the women in my life and make shit happen. I was gon' rule my turf with an iron fist like I was supposed to. I respected Taurus for giving me that entrance into the game, and I was gon' do everything that I could to get my bearings so I could be the one giving the speeches.

He looked out of his driver's side window into the night, just as the rain started to come down in a drizzle. "I think my daughter likes you, Shemar, but I can't have y'all fuckin' around like that because yo' life is finna be the slums. I don't want her caught up in that shit. She loves hard, just like her mother, and I know how this shit go. Pussy finna come a dime a dozen, and my lil' girl— once she get attached— ain't gon' be able to handle that pain. So, I'm asking you as a man to not go there with her unless you know you gon' be one hundred to her through and through. I can't say what I will or won't do if she's brought to tears over a nigga, man. My temper just ain't right when it comes to her and her mom." He smiled and then looked over at me. "So, just so you and I stay on the up and up, just don't go there with her, period. Cool?"

I didn't even know what he was talking about because I had not spoken to Jahliya since the last time we were all in the sewer. I didn't think he had nothing to worry about, and I was guessing that he was just overreacting because she was his little girl, but in that moment, I could respect his wishes. I didn't see nothing forming with her down the road. I just wished I would have been able to see my future and I would have never said to him what I said next.

I nodded. "Yo', big homie. You ain't gotta worry about me messin' with yo' daughter. On my word, I'll never go there with her, and it's all in honor of you."

He extended his hand. "Shake on that as a man and seal this promise amongst gangstas."

I grabbed his hand, looked him straight in the eyes and shook it, sealing our pact.

Before I got out of the car, he tried to hand me a bundle of hundreds. It had to be about twenty thousand dollars.

I pushed his hand away and declined his offer. "I'm good, big homie. I ain't with taking no handouts. I'ma hit that pavement, just like I'm supposed to, and get it for myself. I feel like you've done enough."

He shook his head. "This ain't for you, lil' bruh. You see them faces in that window, up there?" He nodded toward my house.

I looked up and saw Purity and Simone looking out of the window with the curtain peeled back. They looked anxious and a bit worried. I didn't know what was going on. "Yeah, I see 'em."

"You gon' take this money and spoil them Queens, man. Because, at the end of the day, it's what it's all about. This twenty-some bands. You don't owe me shit. Just bless them Queens and always keep them first. Everything else will follow.

You understand that?" He moved his head so he could see out of my side of the car better.

Simone and Purity must've peeped that they were being watched, because in one swift instant the curtain was replaced and they disappeared.

Taurus handed me the money again. "Don't insult me like that, lil' homie. Take this money and cherish our Queens. There is no greater gift to the world more than the black woman. Cherish them and our world becomes stronger." He started the car back up after I took the money. "I want Vito's heart cut out and brought to me. He vouched for that nigga Flyy, so it all comes down on his head, just like whatever you do wrong comes down on mine. The game is cold. Body that nigga and get that heart to me. In less than a week, I'm gon' introduce you to the slums of Cloverland as only a boss can."

Ghost

Chapter 13

As soon as I got into the house, Purity bum-rushed me, knocking Simone out of the way and into the wall. She ran up to me and wrapped her arms around my neck, kissing my lips, and laying her head on my chest while Simone mugged the back of her head with hatred. "I missed you so much, Shemar. I was worried about you." She smacked me on the chest playfully, but enough so that it still hurt. "Why you ain't answer your phone?"

I gave her a hug and tried to break away from her, but she would not let me go. "I was out handling some business. You already know when I'm taking care of somethin', I always leave my phone off until I'm done." I hugged her a lil' tighter, then once again, tried to let her go, but she wasn't going.

"Well, I don't like when you do me like that. I be needing you all the time, and if I can't be with you physically, then I at least want to hear your voice. I can't function without knowing that you're okay."

I kissed her on the forehead. "I know, lil' sis. That's my bad."

Simone walked over, holding her stomach. She stopped on the side of us and mugged, first Purity, and then me. "I need to talk to you, Shemar, seriously." She looked pissed off.

I nodded and tried once again to release Purity from my grasp, but she just held on to me tighter until I looked down at her. "Let me go, sis so I can go and see what Simone want. It shouldn't take that long."

She held me tighter and scrunched her face. "Hell n'all. You ain't always gotta jump when she act like she needing you so bad. Just like she waited for you all day and night, I did the same thing. So, what makes her needs more important than anybody else's?" She mugged Simone and turned her nose up at her.

Simone exhaled and flared her nostrils. "Purity, you really trying my patience right now. Damn. The reason why I need him so bad is because I'm carrying his fuckin' baby, and you just being one." She balled up her fists. "Now, can I talk to my baby daddy without you hanging all over him all of the fucking time? Damn!"

Purity pushed me away and jumped into Simone's face. "Keep cussin' at me, Simone, and I swear to God I'ma kick yo' black ass. I don't give a care what you got growin' inside of you that's supposed to be his. I'm his real sister, so my needs come before yours for always. Get that shit through yo' head." She stepped further into her face and frowned. "You think you ballin' up them fists mean anything to me? Huh?"

Simone lowered her head and took a step back, holding her stomach once again. "You know what, Purity? I'm not gon' go there with you. You're right. You are his blood sister and your needs should come before mine and his baby's." At saying the last part, she looked up at me with glossy eyes. "Shemar, when you get a second, can you please come and holla at me? I just need a few moments of yo' time. Please." She walked off with her head down.

I was about to follow her when Purity blocked my path, and hugged me tight. "Damn, she be getting on my nerves." She took my hand and pulled me toward our room while I watched Simone enter into hers with her head down before closing the door. Once inside of our room, she stood on her tippy toes and kissed my lips for a long time, while I held her waist and listened to her moan deep within her throat.

I wanted to push her away to go and see what was going on with Simone, but I felt it was smarter to tend to Purity first, or else there would have been a big ass scene. After the kiss, I sat down on the love seat that was in our room, and sat her on my lap, holding her with one arm wrapped around her waist. "Look, Purity, you know that sooner or later I'll go in there and see what's good with her because she really do have my kid. I can't keep shitting on her every time, and you gotta start to honor her slot as my child's mother. Y'all gotta get along because we're all family."

Purity jerked her head back as if she were offended. "No, we're not. I don't care about neither one of them like that. Maybe Vicki, a little bit, because she went and got custody of me so I could be with you. But that's as far as it goes. I love you, Shemar, and I don't want to share you with them. I'm insane over you. I'll kill them bitches. That's on our mom." She jumped out of my lap and looked angry as she paced in front of me. "All that bitch got over me is yo' kid. If I had yo' baby growing inside of me instead of the fuckin' Deacon or his son, then you wouldn't have no reason to fuck with that bitch. Shit!" She shook her head and continued to mumble to herself while she paced the floor.

I got up and snatched her lil' ass up, holding her by the shoulder. "Purity, you good, shawty. Stop tryin' to compete with Simone, because I love you the most. I keep on telling you this."

She hugged me. "Then don't go say shit to that bitch tonight, Shemar. Stay in here and hold me all night. Just wrap me in your arms and make me feel better, because I need you more than she ever will. You're mine and that bitch needs to know that." She laid her head on my chest and started to cry.

I took a step back and held her out at arm's length, looking into her face. "Purity, apart of being a man is standing up to my responsibilities. Now, I got her pregnant and I gotta make sure that she straight at all times. I don't know what she wanna talk to me about, but I'm about to go in there and find out. I owe her that much, and it ain't got nothin' to do with you, or against you. I just have to be a man and stand on mine."

Purity looked at me for a long time with tears streaming down her cheeks. Just seeing her cry made me feel sick and frustrated at the same time. I felt sick because I hated to see my lil' sister in any kinds of pain. I always wanted to heal her, and protect her from pain at all costs. I felt frustrated because I felt like she was becoming way too attached. We needed to back up a lil' bit and establish that we were still brother and sister, and not husband and wife. I didn't know what to do. I felt like no matter what I did, somebody was going to be hurt which is why we had to move out of that house. It was becoming too much for me.

Purity wiped away her tears, and walked toward me. "But you aren't going to stay with her all night, right? I mean, you'll come back in here and hold me like I need you to? Can you plant lil' kisses on my neck, and make me feel special as only you can?" She blinked and more tears fell down her cheeks.

The longer I stared at her, the sicker I became on the stomach. I felt like I was killing my sister, and I didn't want to do that. I stepped forward and pulled her into my embrace, wiping away her tears and then kissing her cheeks. "I love you, Purity, and I'll do anything for you. I'll be in here in a minute to hold You, and take care of you in any way that you need me to. You're my angel, and nothing or nobody matters to me more than you do, baby, I promise."

She looked up and kissed my lips, then a smile came over her face while she sniffed back snot. "Okay, Shemar, that sounds cool." She took a step back and pulled down her jogging pants, stepping out of them to expose the fact that she wore red laced panties underneath. Then, she pulled her tank top over her head, reached in front of herself and unsnapped her bra, releasing her breasts with the huge nipples. Finally, she climbed on the bed and looked over her shoulder at me. "You hurry back so you can hold me and whatever else you can think of." She crawled across the bed on all fours.

I couldn't help but to look at the way her thong was all up in her ass. The crotch area was packed with her pussy lips. I hated myself for getting turned on by her antics, but I did. I almost said forget what Simone wanted and jumped in the bed with her so I could be in that body again. But I channeled the lil' self-control that I did have, and closed the door behind me.

I walked down the hall to Simone's room and knocked on the door.

"Who is it?" I heard her ask in a raspy voice as if she was crying.

"It's Shemar. Open the door, girl," I whispered, looking over my shoulder. I was wondering where my mother was. I had not see her the entire day.

Simone pulled the door opened, and stood to the side for me to walk into the room. Once all the way in, she closed the door behind me and sucked her teeth. "I'm surprised she let you come down here. I thought y'all was finna be in the room all night, hugged up." She rolled her eyes and sat on the bed next to me.

She was playing Sam Smith through her phone. I nodded to it because I didn't know what else to do. I knew we was about to argue, but I really didn't want to go there with her. I had a lot of love for Simone, and I could see myself being with her as her man. It was just that I loved Purity so much and my sister was needy. That made things difficult for me and Simone.

I pulled her up until she was standing in front of me with her white boy shorts and pink beater on. Her nipples were threatening to bust through the material. I always loved her lil' thick body. I reached up and stroked her soft cheeks. She pushed her face to the side to feel my hand more.

"What's the matter, baby?"

She swallowed, tilted her head back, and open her eyes wide to keep from crying. "Your sister, Shemar. That's what the problem is." She shook her head and swallowed again. "I don't understand why she

wanna hog you all to herself when I got your baby."
Her voice was breaking up. "I feel like you forgetting
about me, ever since she been here. I wanna die." She
turned her back to me and leaned her head down with
her hands covering her face. "I didn't know it was
going to be like this." Now she was breaking down
in full tears.

I felt sicker than somebody with the flu. I never
wanted to hurt Simone. Me and her had been through
a lot, just like me and Purity. I pulled her back around
so she was facing me. "Simone, baby, I'm sorry. I'm
doing all that I can to juggle everything, but I'm just
failing, baby. Please don't cry, because I need your
strength right now."

She cried harder and fell into me. I had to wrap
my arms around her. "Shemar, I love you so much. I
would give my life for you in a heartbeat. Don't
nothin' matter in this world to me, if it ain't you.
You're my everything, and you always have been.
Now you're going to leave me because of yo' sister.
It just sucks." She cried into the crux of my neck, and
further broke my heart.

I'm one of those dudes who can't take it when a
female cries. That shit kills my soul and I will do anything to make it stop and to make them feel better.
I've always been that way, and still am to this day.

I held her in my arms and felt my throat get tight.
"Simone, I love you, baby. You're mine; do you hear
me? You need to stay strong for our baby that is
growing inside of you. I'm so sorry, baby. I promise
to be better and to try harder. All you have to do is
tell me what you need from me. Please, ma."

She shook her head. "I just want you to love me for real. I want you to be here for me. Hold me. Tell me how special I am. Show me that I mean more to you than just some chick that is pregnant with your child. Put me first. Me and your unborn child. Can you do that, Shemar?"

I looked down at her with my eyes getting watery, for some reason. I knew that I was fuckin' up, but I didn't know how to get everything back the way it needed to be. I was struggling to figure things out. My mother needed me, and I had to be there for her in every single way, because she had sacrificed so much for me, including her marriage. Purity had been through so much that I just had to heal her in every way that I possibly could, because she was my responsibility and I was all that she had in this world. She demanded a lot of me, but who was I to not step up to the plate and give all of them to her. Nikki needed me to be there for her in every way that I could, and since I had been the only male in her life since we were kids, I knew that I could never not be all that she needed me to be. Then, Simone and our unborn child needed me. I was obligated to be there for her at all costs. I knew that only a chump wouldn't be there for his kid and the mother. I was more of a man than that. I had to make her my priority. I had to figure things out and get better control of my lower region, because at that time I didn't have much sexual control of myself, and that would wind up being my downfall.

"Simone, you deserve for me to put you first. Ever since you been in my life, you ain't been nothin' but one hundred to me. I hate seeing you cry, especially with me knowing that I'm the cause of it. So, even though you gotta know that I'm not perfect, I'm gon' try my best to get better so I can be all that you need for me to be. But you gotta give me that wiggle room. Let me figure things out, slowly but surely. If you'll do that, in time, I'll be what I'm supposed to be to you."

She blinked tears, then came and hugged me with her chest rising and falling. "I love you so much, Shemar. I don't want to stress you out. I know you got a lot on your plate, and I know that yo' sister is real needy. I just need to know that you'll be there for me and the baby when it gets here. I don't know if I can play second fiddle to Purity forever. I'm not mentally strong enough to endure such things as that." She snuggled her face into my chest. "I need you at the OBGYN with me tomorrow, too. I would be sick if you're not beside me, Shemar. So, you have to be."

I sat down on the bed before laying all the way back and pulling her on top of me. She spread her legs and had each thigh on either side of me, just laying there while I rubbed her back.

I had a lil' thing for Simone. I honestly did love her, and I kinda wanted to be with her on some one on one shit because I felt like she deserved a consistent father in her and our child's life. I was gon' try as hard as I possibly could to be that father. I mean, I knew I was gon' make a lot of mistakes along the way, but I still had to try and do the best I could. I owed them that.

She straddled me, then leaned down and kissed my lips before turning her head to the side and rubbing her face against my lips, with her eyes closed. "Mmm. I just love the feel of you. I can't wait to see what we look like together inside of one body. I know our baby gon' be fine, and I hope he get your hazel eyes. That'll be a blessing." She smiled and kissed me again while I palmed her big booty and tried to imagine her having my kid.

Even though I knew she really was pregnant I still could not imagine how things were going to be one hundred percent. I couldn't imagine me having a child that looked up to me as their father. I was about to step knee deep into the streets and I just worried that my clock would be punched before my kid could even be born. I thought about my death every single day. I just felt like it was more near than further away. I wasn't afraid to go. I just wanted to make sure that when I went that I left my people in a financially stable position. I knew that I was their sacrifice.

Simone sat all the way up and looked into my face. "Shemar, was you really serious when you was saying how much you love me and stuff? Or was you just trying to get me to stop crying?" She ran her hands over my chest, squeezing my pecks, then looking me straight in the eyes.

I sat up just a lil' bit. "I meant every word that I said. I really do love you, Simone. I always have. Me and you been through a lot together, ever since I came to live with you and mom. You're deep in my heart, and I'll kill a muhfucka over you, quick. That's my word."

"Awww-a." Her bottom lip quivered before she leaned all the way over and kissed me again. She bucked her ass backward into my roaming hands.

I was squeezing and massaging that big ass booty. Trailing my hand all the way down to the leg holes, I threatened to slide my finger under the material. Her cat sat right in the middle with heat radiating from it.

She sucked on my neck and then bit into it with force. "I love you so much, Shemar. You drive me all the way crazy. I want you to give me some real quick before yo' sister interrupt us. Come on." She slid off of me and started to pull her boy shorts down her ankles, and all the way off of her feet. Then, she kicked them across the room and slid her beater over her head, exposing her pretty titties with the brown the nipples.

I got undressed right away, and she jumped on me. She squeezed my dick in her hand, and pulled back the skin of it before sliding the head into her hot asshole. She didn't waste no time riding me like a jockey at full speed while she closed her eyes and had her head tilted back, with her face toward the ceiling. That pussy felt so good that I started to make noises while I held that ass.

"Shemar. Mmm. Mmm. Mmm. Unnnn. Shit. Shemar. You so deep. Mmmm. I want you to cum in me so bad." She rode me faster and faster. Her titties bounced on her chest.

"Huh. Get it, baby. Fuck daddy, baby. Make me cum in you. Come on now," I encouraged, pulling her breast down so I could suck back and forth on each hard nipple.

I loved her titties. Her nipples drove me insane. They always had, and so did her mother's.

Simone leaned forward and grabbed the headboard for leverage. Then she got to bouncing up and down on me like a bounce house. My dick went in and out of that tight pussy while it sucked at me for dear life. It was wet, and searing me. It was so good that I couldn't hold back that long.

As soon as she started quaking and shivering all over me, I felt her pussy spitting its juices against my dick. Then, she leaned down and bit into my shoulder while her hips continued to fuck me harder and harder.

I couldn't take it no more. "I'm cumming, Simone. I'm cumming in this pussy, baby. here I cum. Huhhhhhh!" I clenched my teeth as my milk got to squirting deep within her kitty.

She shrieked, bit me harder and started to cum with her whole body shaking. "Shemar! Shemar! hhh-shit, daddy!" Her hips worked faster, then she was cumming all over me.

I flipped her onto her back and put her thick thighs to her breasts. I was finna tear this pregnant pussy up, but then there was a beating on her room door.

Chapter 14

Simone didn't even put up a fight. She knew who it was at the door. She slowly slid from under me, got under her covers and told me that she hoped I would keep my word, and that she would see me in the morning. She told me to go and cater to Purity, that she was happy that she had gotten a lil' piece of me. It meant more than the world to her.

While Purity continued to knock on the door, I tongued her down then told her that I loved her. Ten minutes later, I was climbing in my bed behind Purity as she held the covers open for me to get in.

She looked over her shoulder. "I know you just fucked that bitch, Shemar, but that don't mean that I don't get none of you tonight. You're supposed to be mine first, and hers and everybody else's second." She scooted back until her naked ass was in my lap.

It was hot and felt soft and enticing. Don't ask me how I was able to go from one room into the next, because I couldn't tell you. It was like every room, and every person was a different situation that affected me, in a certain way. I felt like I needed to be there for them all, and I didn't know who I was gon' wind up with. I was so lost and confused.

But when Purity reached behind her and took my dick, and slid it into her pussy again, while we laid on our side, I couldn't do nothing but pick up her right thigh and slow-stroke that cat while she moaned deep within her throat. Her cat felt a little more snug than Simone's. Not by much, but I could tell the difference. She also appeared to be two times more wet. I got to hitting that shit for real, listening to the music of her moans.

"Ummm. Tell me you love me, Shemar. Tell me that I'm the one you love the most again. I need to hear it."

I moved in and out of her pussy at a steady pace— hitting her bottom, then pulling all the way back just to stab forward again and smash that cat. Her scent was intoxicating and I couldn't even tell you why. I think I just had that forbidden shit in me real bad, and Purity catered to that animal part of me.

I sucked on her tittie. "I love you, baby. I love you the most. You're my angel. I mean that."

"Uhhh!" She bounced back into me harder. "Tell me more. Please-a. I love your voice, Shemar." She reached behind her and dug her nails into the side of my ass cheek, while I plowed in and out of that pussy, harder and harder.

"I love you, baby. You're my angel. You're my everything. Huh. Huh. Huh. I love you so much. Damn, I love you." I sped up the pace and got to killing it with all of my might.

She grabbed the pillow and bit into it, screaming as loud as as she could. Our skins slapped together and sounded like somebody was clapping their hands together. "I'm cumming, big bruh. I'm cumming on yo' dick. Uhhh. It feels so good. It feel. So. So. Gooood. Uhhhh-a!" She smashed her ass back into me with all of her might, and I slammed forward meeting her stroke for stroke.

Since I had already cum with Simone, I felt like I could go all night, and I damn near did. I hit that pussy until Purity begged me to stop and let her go to sleep, and that's just what I did.

The next morning, after I stepped out of the shower and got fitted in Gucci, I opened the door to the bathroom, and there was my mother standing in front of the door with a big smile on her face. I looked her up and down like she was crazy, while I brushed my waves and rubbed the top of my head with my hand, feeling my wave pattern get deeper.

"I got you, son. You know momma would never fail you, and I got you." She smiled real big and grabbed my hand, pulling me into her room and closing the door behind us.

As soon as it was closed, she picked up a Louis Vuitton bag and turned it upside down, dumping bundles of cash out of it and onto her bed. My eyes were as big as paper plates.

"You told me you needed a hundred thousand dollars and I got it for you. It took me some time, but I made it happen. Are you happy, baby?" She looked over to me with a worried look on her face. It was the first time in a long time that I had seen her without makeup on. She looked beautiful, but at the same time, tired and stressed out. I could tell that she had not slept in a few days because there were bags under her eyes. "Say something, dear."

I walked to the bed and picked up the money, bundle by bundle. "Dang, momma, what you have to do to get all of this?" I looked over to her and she looked off, avoiding my eyes. "I can't hear you," I said, grabbing her chin and making her face me.

She slightly yanked her head away from me, and turned her back on me, walking over to the lone love seat in her room. She plopped down in it and crossed her big thighs. "I just got from Vincent what I was supposed to get a long time ago. All he gon' do is go and spend it on his other family anyway. I might as well get what I'm deserved and give it to my baby. Now, just tell momma you happy and we ain't gon' worry about it." She stood up and walked over to me as I thumbed through the hundreds, placing her hands on my upper back, and rubbing my shoulders.

I nodded and started to stuff the money back in the bag. "Momma, I ain't even gon' lie to you. I forgot that I even told you to get this for me because I went out there and made things happen on my own. You already knew I wasn't gon' sit still. You raised me better than that." After putting all of the money back in the bag, I turned around and tried to hand it to her. "Here."

She scrunched her face and pushed the bag away. "Hell n'all, Shemar. I got that for you because you're my little man, and I need to know that you still need me in some sort of way. I went out into them streets and made it happen for you because that's my job when it comes to you. You think you're going to re-pay me by throwing it back into my face after all that shit that I done? Oh hell no. You can burn that money in the fireplace in the front room for all I care, but you're going to give me my credit. Now, hug me, boy. Now!" She opened her arms, looking me over with anger written across her face.

I held the bag in my hand, not moving. Just look-ing back at her. I didn't know what to say or do in that moment. I mean, she did have to completely cross out the Pastor in order to make that happen for me, so I guessed that I did owe her some form of gratitude for that. I didn't like arguing with my mother either, and unlike my sisters, when my mother got emotional, she mostly expressed anger and got physical. It wasn't that I couldn't handle her or I was worried about her beating me, or nothing, because I wasn't. I just felt like she needed to know that I appreciated her making it happen for me. So, once again, I played my role. That was the one thing about having so many women in my life to tend too. Everybody needed me to play some sort of role, so much so that I didn't know which character was the actual me anymore. I was pretty much filling in the blanks as needed; me being the only man of their lives and all.

I tossed the bag of money on the bed and walked into her arms, hugging her, and kissing her on the neck, before sucking on it a lil' bit to emphasize my appreciation of her. She loved whenever I did that. "I love you, momma, and I appreciate you for going out of this house and making it happen for yo' lil' boy, as only you could. You're so special to me, which is why I will never leave you and I will always need you."

She shuddered and held on to me tighter. "You know I love to hear you talk like that, baby. It drives momma crazy. I love my lil' man so much." She bit into my neck and sucked on it super hard and loud, sending shivers through me.

After messing around with Simone and Purity, my dick was sore. Even if I wanted to make love to her. there was no way I was going to be able to. Her sucking had got me hard, and I was in serious pain. Then, when she reached between us and squeezed my pipe, I wanted to cry.

My eyes got watery. "Mmm, momma. I love you too," I said through clenched teeth, and with my eyes closed because of the pain from too much sex.

She licked my neck and sucked on my earlobe. "You wanna show momma how thankful you are, baby? I need you to put me to sleep so bad. I deserve it." She started to unbuckle my Gucci belt.

I was so happy when Purity knocked on the door twice then let herself in.

My mother jumped back and turned around, walking toward the love seat in her room. When she turned around, I noticed that both of her nipples were hard and straining to buss through her Lord and Taylor blouse. She had a frown on her face. "Purity, don't you know how to wait until somebody invites you into their room? Huh?"

Purity gave her a look that said she wanted to snap out at her, but she caught herself and took a deep breath. "My bad, Vicki. I just needed to tell Shemar that Nikki is out here and she say she need him right away, That's all." She looked over to me with a jealous look on her face before looking back at my mother. "I think it's an emergency. Come on, Shemar. You can always talk to Vicki later." She opened the door wide enough for me to step past her, and I was just about to do that when my mother grabbed my wrist and waved Purity off.

"He'll be out there in a second, Purity. Tell Nikki to give him a few minutes while we get an understanding amongst ourselves. Go." She walked toward the door, and when she got to it, she started to close it.

Purity scrunched her face and backed away. "Dang. Well, hurry up, Shemar. Don't keep her waiting. It could be an emergency."

Before she could get the last part out, my mother closed the door in her face and locked it. She backed me up into the wall and attacked my neck, while rubbing all over my stomach muscles. "Mmm. Tonight, baby, me and you going to a hotel or something, so you can spend a few hours in this pussy. Do you hear me? I need you to go savage mode on me like I taught you. I deserve it." She kissed my lips again, and we started tonguing each other down.

I was so happy that I didn't have to fuck her right then. I needed a lil' break, and the fact that she was hollering that she didn't want none of me until later was a relief. So, I tongued her down, then picked her up and threw her on the bed. She landed on her back with her legs wide open, sliding her hand into her panties while she licked her lips and lowered her eyes at me.

I nodded. "Just me and you tonight, ma. I got you. Thank you for making it happen for me."

She pulled her panties to the side, exposing her sex lips, sliding her finger up and down her crease. "N'all, baby, save your thank you's for tonight, because that's when I'm gon' need 'em."

When I got into the living room, Simone and Nikki were sitting across from each other, engaged in conversation. When I walked up, all I heard was Nikki say, "And you sure its Shemar baby?"

Simone stood up and looked down at her with anger written across her face. "Why would you even ask me something like that? I mean, who else baby could it be?"

Nikki stood up with her face scrunched. "Look, home girl, I'm just making sho my nigga ain't being played. I know how hoes get down, and I ain't honoring that when it comes to him. You actin' like you got an attitude and all that shit, but this ain't that. What you talking about?" Nikki took out a .44 Desert Eagle and sat it on the table, before throwing her hair into a pony tail.

I jumped in the middle of them right away. I knew Nikki was nothing like Purity. She would kill Simone, or at the very least beat our baby out of her, because she ain't like her being pregnant no way. So, I had to break that stuff up before it got too far.

I wrapped my arm around Simone and walked toward her bedroom with her. "Come on, baby, you need to chill out and just leave her alone because yall beefing ain't gon' help none of us."

I looked over my shoulder to see Nikki picking back up her pistol and putting it in the small of her back. "Yeah, Shemar, you betta tell ol' girl what this is. We in blood in, nigga. This shit deeper than foster families." She sat back on the couch as Purity walked past us, mugging Simone.

"You should've let they ass fight. You can't always save her irritating ass." She walked into the living room and hugged Nikki.

Soon as we got into Simone's room, she broke down to her knees, crying. I felt horrible. I got down on my knees, holding her until she calmed down. I rubbed her back the whole time, then she said something that scared the shit out of me.

"Shemar, its like ain't none of these bitches gon' let me have you to myself. They just gon' keep on bringing this drama until I'm out of the picture. They just don't know how much I love you, and how loyal I am to you. I'm the only one that know you killed the Deacon and his family. I'm the only one, and I ain't tell the police nothing. I kept my mouth shut because I need you by my side. But it seems like I ain't ever gon' be able to have you all to myself. So, now, I don't know what to do." Her eyes got bucked and she stared off into space while tears ran down her cheeks.

My heart was beating so fast that I couldn't breathe. I was trying to decide if she had just threatened me in a nonchalant sort of way. I wanted to lose my temper, and for the first time I started to feel leery with her. "Simone, what you just say?"

She pursed her lips and turned to me, looking me in the face. "Shemar, I know you killed the three Robinsons so yo' sister could come and live with us. I'm not stupid, even though I play the fool at times." She stood up and sat on her bed, looking out of her window, out into the rainy night.

I felt like I was ready to throw up. That was three murders, and now I was eighteen which meant that I was going straight with the big boys on death row. My head was spinning so fast that I was at a loss for words. "Simone, what you trying to say, huh?" I stood in front of her and tilted her chin up to me. "You tryna say that you finna get the police involved, so you can blame they murders on me or somethin'?"

She scrunched her face and smacked my hand away. "Nigga, what's yo' fuckin problem? What I look like getting you popped off? I don't get down like that, and me and you way better than that. I was just bringing that up to match what Nikki was saying about y'alls loyalty. I think that me and yours run deeper because I know more than she do." She took a deep breath and exhaled loudly. "Huh-a! Why can't these hoes just leave you alone? I want you to myself. We growin' a whole ass baby together. Don't that matter for anything?"

Just then, Nikki knocked on the door and stuck her head inside of the room. "Shemar, we gotta go and handle that one situation right now. Nut just hit my phone on some urgent biz. So, wrap this shit up and let's go." She tapped her female Rolex watch. "Time is money."

I nodded, and kneeled in front of Simone after Nikki closed the door back. "Look, Simone, I ain't ever lied to you before and I don't want to start. I won't get into what you talking about in regards to the Robinsons, because you need to stay out of that. But what I will say is that I love you, baby, and we gone figure all of this stuff out together. In the end, it's gon' be me, and you I can assure you of that. You just gotta let me get things in order. Be patient, and let's keep fighting for each other. Okay?"

She smiled, looking down at me. "Okay, baby, but we need to break away from here soon. I need you all to myself, and so does our baby when it gets here. But for now, go and handle yo' business. I'll be here waiting for you when you get home."

I stood up and lifted up her shirt, kissing her stomach. "We gone figure it out, baby. Just give us time to. I love you."

"I love you too, Shemar, and I trust you. The question is, do you trust. But the question is, do you really trust me?"

In that moment, I didn't know if I really did or not, and I was struggling with the information that she had just given me about the knowledge of the Robinson family murders. I really didn't know what to do, or how to feel, but once again, I had never lied to her, and I didn't intend on doing it right then, even though I probably should have.

"Honestly, Simone, I trust you, but I don't know to what extent. I guess only time a tell."

Tears fell out of her eyes as she looked at me for a long time without saying a word. "Yeah, I guess it will."

Ghost

Chapter 15

An hour later, me and Nikki were rolling out to go and meet up with Nut. On the way, I told her everything about the Robinson's murders, including the bomb that Simone had just dropped on me about knowing about them. As soon as I said the last part, she was heated.

"Nigga, you stupid. That bitch too emotional to have that info. You gotta let me kill that bitch, or I promise you gon' be in prison real soon. Trust me when I tell you that. That bitch gotta know you fuckin' Purity and her mother. Then, I'm in the mix and she don't know what we doing. Sometimes, for a female, it's just easier to know that if she can't have you all to herself, that nobody else can either. So, you're better off in prison somewhere, because out of sight, out of mind. I gotta stank her ass quick."

I ain't gon' even lie and say that her words weren't freaking me out, because they were. I knew that Nikki understood females in a way that I never could. So, who was I to question what she was getting at? But I also had to keep in mind that Nikki was very overprotective of me, and she didn't like the fact that Simone was carrying my baby. I felt like she wanted to find a way to get rid of her anyway, and now that she knew Simone had information on three murders that I had committed, she was gon' use it to body her ass.

Before I could let her know what was on my mind, she pulled her Lexus up in front of Nut, who ran from the side of an abandoned house and jumped in the back of the car with his hood on. "Yo', it took yo ass long enough, Nikki. You told me ten minutes. That was an hour ago."

Nikki rolled her eyes and pulled off. "Blame that shit on Shemar. He had to peel a bitch off of him before he got in my whip." She laughed to herself.

Nut put his hand on my shoulder. "Peace, god."

I nodded. "Peace. So, what's the deal with this nigga Vito, man?"

He coughed and covered his mouth. "Sun at this pool hall over on Ashland Street. I guess he doing some deal in there with some Mexicans from the Northside. They like ten deep altogether. I don't know how long the meeting gon' last, but that shit don't matter, because as soon as them Mexicans come out, we going in. I got us some vests and shit, too. Nikki, pull into that alley over there."

She nodded and turned down the SZA track that was playin' on her radio. "A'iight. Damn, I feel all jittery and shit. I ain't wet nothin' up in a minute, and I been hatin' that nigga Vito. So, I'ma enjoy this shit."

She pulled into the next alley, got half way down it, and parked, turning off her headlights while the rain started to come down harder. Being that it was late April, Houston was getting a lot of rain at this time.

Nut handed me a vest that had FBI written across the chest, and gave Nikki a smaller one that said the same thing.

I looked over my shoulder at him. "Where you get these muhfuckas from?" I took my shirts off and slid it onto my frame, making sure that I was putting it on right.

Nikki took her Fendi top off, and slid her vest in place. "He got these bitches from Taurus. They been talking since you been in that house playin' Hugh Hefner and shit." She snickered. "Only yo' ass, Shemar." She shook her head and continued to fit her vest on.

I wasn't finna get into no dumb shit with her right then. I was trying to wrap my head around what we were getting ready to do. Taurus said that he wanted Vito's heart, and it was my only way into the game. I was down to get it by any means because I was feening for my portion of the slums. I felt like I was born for it, and whatever Taurus needed me to do so that him and Hood Rich could stand tall behind me, I was gon' do it to the best of my ability.

After I got my vest in place, I slid my black Gucci back over it and took my ski mask out of my pocket. Nikki had hers laying on her lap. She pulled an Uzi from under her seat, took the clip out, looked it over, and slammed it back in place before setting it on her lap again.

Nut reached over my shoulder and handed me a Tech .9 with an extended clip. "Say, Kid, you ready to chop some shit down or what? You been awfully quiet up there."

I nodded. "I'm ready, nigga. Let me ask you a question, though. After we hit this last lick, what you gon' do? You gon' stay down here in Houston, or you riding back out to New York?"

He shrugged. "That just depends on if y'all want me down here or not, Kid. I mean, have I overstayed my welcome?"

I shook my head. "Never that, nigga. Once I get the key to the streets, I'm gon' need that New York shit in my army."

Nikki ran her finger across her teeth while she looked in the rear-view mirror. "Yeah, cuzz, you good. We about to turn Cloverland out, and I feel like you should be a part of it since you been handling business beside my right hand after I went down. That nigga got love for you, I can tell, which is odd because he hate all niggas. Trust me."

Nut curled his upper lip. "Then it's settled. I'm here, Kid. All I ask is that I can bring my lil' branch of Brooklyn niggas down here and I can get my piece of the pie, too. We'll really turn this bitch out. Word is bond."

I ain't have no problem with that, and I made sure I let the homie know that once I got in the game that he had the green light to bring as many savages from New York as he wanted to. I wanted to build a nation under me and set the city on fire.

Twenty minutes later, the rain was pouring down so hard that it sounded like hail on top of our stolen Dodge Caravan. We pulled up and parked two car spaces away from Ashland's pool hall. We knew that Vito and the Mexicans had to be inside 'cause in front of the pool hall were two Benz trucks, sitting on gold rims, with illusion paint jobs. In front of those whips was a cherry 1964 Impala fully laced, with gold rims and tinted windows. I knew from experience that the Essays loved riding around in '64's. For what reason, I couldn't tell you, but in Houston it was just their thing.

I rolled down my mask and cocked back my tech. Then, I looked over at Nikki just as she got her mask in place. "Nikki, you make sure you come through the door last. Let me and Nut do our thing, then once we open that bitch up, you can come in and let them muhfuckas have it. What you think about that?" I asked, watching the door of the pool hall.

Nikki sucked her teeth. "Nigga, since when am I waiting in the weeds while all of the hard work get taken care of?" She shook her head. "You got me fucked up. You know how I get down, Shemar. Don't try and flex on me in front of my cousin, because he already know what it is, just like you do." She straightened her mask. "I'll go in there with one of y'all, and one of you niggas can come in once all of the hard work is done."

I shook my head. "Damn, Nikki, I wasn't even sayin' it like that. I was just trying to protect yo' ass 'cause you just caught a bunch of slugs a few weeks ago. You ain't gotta be on the frontlines, provin' shit to nobody. We already know you just as much of a gangsta as we is."

Soon as I finished saying that, I saw the pool hall's door open, and two Mexicans came out of it, holding briefcases in their hands. They walked up to the '64, opened the doors and got in, before speeding away from the curb. They got to the lights at the top of the intersection and made a left, storming away.

I felt butterflies come into my stomach, then my heartbeat sped up because it was time to get the show on the road. Vito had to be inside, and we needed to hit him up and get shit over and done with.

"Say, Kid, look. Why don't me and Nikki run in this bitch then, god? And you can come in directly after us. Hit anything that might get away from our first slugs. I mean, 'cause it don't matter what two go in there, just as long as we get the job done," Nut said, fixing his mask in place.

By this time, I really didn't care who went in first or how we got the job done, just as long as we did. Vito was the last hit on the list and I needed to make this happen so I could bully my way into Cloverland.

"That sound cool, bruh. Let's just make this shit happen so we can get this nigga heart back to Taurus."

Nut opened the back door and prepared to get out. "Sound like a muthafuckin plan to me, Kid, let's. Get it." He jumped out of the van and crouched low to the ground as lightning flashed across the sky, and thunder roared overhead.

A few seconds later, Nikki opened her door and was on the side of him as they stayed close on the side of a furniture store that was right next to the pool hall. I was just about to get out of the van as well when my phone vibrated. I was about to look at it, but something told me to check it real fast. I just had a nagging in my gut, so I did and the text I read nearly made me want to abort the mission and get home.

The text was from Simone and it said, *"Shemar, get home quick. My father's in their room, killing my mother. Please don't ignore. This is not a joke."*

Just as I was about to call her straight through so I could find out what was going on, Nut opened the door to the pool hall and ran inside with Nikki right behind him. I heard the gunshots almost immediately.

"Fuck!"

I threw the phone in my pocket and jumped out of the van, running full speed to the pool hall's door, and swinging it open in time to see Nikki hit up a real fat, bald nigga who had on a bright ass Coogi sweater. *Boom! Boom! Boom!* Three big ass holes filled his chest, causing him to fall backward and crash into the pool sticks behind him, before falling onto his stomach in a puddle of blood.

There was an old man behind the bar with a big shot gun. He aimed it at Nikki and fired, but not before I could run and push her out of the way. *Boooom!* His bullets slammed into the glass in front of the pool hall, and shattered it. He cocked the big weapon and prepared to shoot again, when Nut let his Tech spit rapidly. *Thot-thot-thot-thot-thot-thot!* The old man inhaled bullets, all in his midsection, before falling to the ground.

"Bitch ass nigga!" Nut hollered.

Another fat nigga came out of the hallway where the bathrooms were, bussing. *Boom! Boom! Boom!*

"Awww!" Nut jerked forward and fell on his chest. "I'm hit, Kid. Fuck!" He turned on his side and bussed toward the hallway.

The fat man ducked down and ran back the way he came.

I hopped up off Nikki and ran in his direction. He stopped and turned around, ducked down, preparing to aim. That's when I let my Tech bark. *Thot-thot-thot-thot-thot-thot-thot-thot!* The bullets flew all in his direction, but none seemed to hit him because he bounced up and bussed three times in my direction, before running through the bathroom door. *Boom! Boom! Boom!*

I ducked behind a pool table and watched as wood flew across the floor as his bullets slammed into the table's side. By this time, Nikki was leaning over Nut, checking on him. He had blood coming through his clothes and looked like he was in severe pain by the way he lay awkwardly on his side.

I looked around and didn't see that nigga Vito nowhere. In fact, the pool hall was empty with the exception of the old man and the two fat niggas. I guessed that Vito had sent them to handle his business for him. He must not have trusted the Mexicans.

In less than a minute after coming to that conclusion, I under stood why, because that same '64 pulled back up in front of the pool hall, but this time, it had two other cars with it. They parked out front, and just as we were helping Nut to his feet, about ten of them jumped out of their whips, heavily armed. They stopped in front of the pool hall and let that muthafucka have it while we were still in there.

Boom! Boom! Boom! Boom! Boom! Boom! Boo-wa! Boo-wa! Boo-wa! Boo-wa! Boom! Boom! Boom! Boom!

Glass shattered all over the place as the wall filled up with holes, and the pool tables were chopped to shreds. I tried to finish helping Nut get to his feet, when I felt a slug fly into my back and knock me all the way forward into the counter.

I fell to my knees as the burning sensation started to sear at me. "I'm hit, Nikki. Fuck, I'm hit, ma."

She jumped up with her Uzi while the shots continued to come at us. "Nooooooo!"

Thaaaaaaaaaaaat! Thaaaaaaaaaat!

She spat fire out at them. I saw two dudes fall to the street, while men on the side of them kept on bussing from their shotguns and Mach .11's. *Boom!* A bullet hit Nikki and knocked her back into me. We fell against the counter on our asses, while Nut laid in the middle of the floor, struggling to breathe.

"Nikki! Nooo! Please! Nikkiii!" I hollered, holding her in my arms while she laid against me with her eyes closed.

Boom! Boom! Boom! Boom! Tissshhhhhi! More glass shattered and flew all around the pool hall. I tried to aim my Tech to buss, but the bullets from them were coming too fast. On top of that, my phone started to vibrate again. I thought about my mother while I held Nikki in my arms. She was unmoving. Nut struggled to get up from the floor, then fell back down with blood dripping from him. The shots continued to come at us.

Boom! Boom! Boom! Boom! Boom! Boom! Boo-wa! Boo-wa! Boo-wa!

Nut jerked forward after being hit again, and fell on his stomach. Now, he was unmoving. One of the Mexicans came forward with an AK47 in his hands. He broke the rest of the glass out of the big window, and stepped through it with a mug on his face. He took the assault rifle and aimed it down at Nut, lowering his eyes.

My phone continued to vibrate in my pocket while my heart beat rapidly in my chest, throbbing and pounding against my ribcage.

Nikki lay in my arms, unmoving. I worried that she was dead. If that was the case, I had failed her again. I just knew that the Mexican was about to empty his clip into Nut, and then come for me and Nikki. But it wouldn't be easy. I grabbed my my Tech and put my finger on the trigger as the Mexican looked down at to Nut, getting ready to blow him away. It was now or never.

To Be Continued...
Bred by the Slums 3
Coming Soon

Stay Connected with Us!

Text **LOCKDOWN** to 22828 to stay
up-to-date with new releases, sneak peaks,
contests and more...

Thank you!

Submission Guideline.

Submit the first three chapters of your completed manuscript to ldpsubmissions@gmail.com, subject line: Your book's title. The manuscript must be in a .doc file and sent as an attachment. Document should be in Times New Roman, double spaced and in size 12 font. Also, provide your synopsis and full contact information. If sending multiple submissions, they must each be in a separate email.

Have a story but no way to send it electronically? You can still submit to LDP/Ca$h Presents. Send in the first three chapters, written or typed, of your completed manuscript to:

LDP: Submissions Dept
Po Box 870494
Mesquite, Tx 75187

DO NOT send original manuscript. Must be a duplicate.

Provide your synopsis and a cover letter containing your full contact information.

Thanks for considering LDP and Ca$h Presents.

Coming Soon from Lock Down Publications/Ca$h Presents

BOW DOWN TO MY GANGSTA

By **Ca$h**

TORN BETWEEN TWO

By **Coffee**

BLOOD STAINS OF A SHOTTA **III**

By **Jamaica**

WHEN THE STREETS CLAP BACK **II**

By **Jibril Williams**

STEADY MOBBIN

By **Marcellus Allen**

BLOOD OF A BOSS **V**

By **Askari**

BRIDE OF A HUSTLA **III**

By **Destiny Skai**

WHEN A GOOD GIRL GOES BAD **II**

By **Adrienne**

THE HEART OF A GANGSTA **III**

By **Jerry Jackson**

LOYAL TO THE GAME **IV**

By **T.J. & Jelissa**

A DOPEBOY'S PRAYER **II**

By **Eddie "Wolf" Lee**

IF LOVING YOU IS WRONG... **III**

Ghost

LOVE ME EVEN WHEN IT HURTS

By **Jelissa**

DAUGHTERS SAVAGE

By **Chris Green**

BLOODY COMMAS **III**

SKI MASK CARTEL II

By **T.J. Edwards**

TRAPHOUSE KING

By **Hood Rich**

BLAST FOR ME **II**

RAISED AS A GOON V

BRED BY THE SLUMS III

By **Ghost**

A DISTINGUISHED THUG STOLE MY HEART **III**

By **Meesha**

ADDICTIED TO THE DRAMA **II**

By **Jamila Mathis**

LIPSTICK KILLAH II

By **Mimi**

THE BOSSMAN'S DAUGHTERS 4

WHAT BAD BITCHES DO

By **Aryanna**

Available Now

RESTRAINING ORDER **I & II**

Bred by the Slums 2

By **CA$H & Coffee**

LOVE KNOWS NO BOUNDARIES **I II & III**

By **Coffee**

RAISED AS A GOON I, II, III & IV

BRED BY THE SLUMS

By **Ghost**

LAY IT DOWN **I & II**

LAST OF A DYING BREED

BLOOD STAINS OF A SHOTTA I & II

By **Jamaica**

LOYAL TO THE GAME

LOYAL TO THE GAME II

LOYAL TO THE GAME III

By **TJ & Jelissa**

BLOODY COMMAS I & II

SKI MASK CARTEL

By **T.J. Edwards**

IF LOVING HIM IS WRONG...I & II

By **Jelissa**

WHEN THE STREETS CLAP BACK

By **Jibril Williams**

A DISTINGUISHED THUG STOLE MY HEART I & II

By **Meesha**

PUSH IT TO THE LIMIT

By **Bre' Hayes**

Ghost

BLOOD OF A BOSS **I, II, III & IV**

By **Askari**

THE STREETS BLEED MURDER **I, II & III**

THE HEART OF A GANGSTA I & II

By **Jerry Jackson**

CUM FOR ME

CUM FOR ME 2

CUM FOR ME 3

An **LDP Erotica Collaboration**

BRIDE OF A HUSTLA **I & II**

THE FETTI GIRLS **I, II& III**

By **Destiny Skai**

WHEN A GOOD GIRL GOES BAD

By **Adrienne**

A GANGSTER'S REVENGE **I II III & IV**

THE BOSS MAN'S DAUGHTERS

THE BOSS MAN'S DAUGHTERS II

THE BOSSMAN'S DAUGHTERS III

A SAVAGE LOVE **I & II**

BAE BELONGS TO ME

A HUSTLER'S DECEIT I, II

By **Aryanna**

A KINGPIN'S AMBITON

A KINGPIN'S AMBITION **II**

I MURDER FOR THE DOUGH

By **Ambitious**

TRUE SAVAGE

TRUE SAVAGE II

TRUE SAVAGE **III**

By **Chris Green**

A DOPEBOY'S PRAYER

By **Eddie "Wolf" Lee**

THE KING CARTEL **I, II & III**

By **Frank Gresham**

THESE NIGGAS AIN'T LOYAL **I, II & III**

By **Nikki Tee**

GANGSTA SHYT **I II &III**

By **CATO**

THE ULTIMATE BETRAYAL

By **Phoenix**

BOSS'N UP **I , II & III**

By **Royal Nicole**

I LOVE YOU TO DEATH

By Destiny J

I RIDE FOR MY HITTA

I STILL RIDE FOR MY HITTA

By **Misty Holt**

LOVE & CHASIN' PAPER

By **Qay Crockett**

TO DIE IN VAIN

Ghost

By **ASAD**

BROOKLYN HUSTLAZ

By **Boogsy Morina**

BROOKLYN ON LOCK I & II

By **Sonovia**

GANGSTA CITY

By **Teddy Duke**

A DRUG KING AND HIS DIAMOND

A DOPEMAN'S RICHES

By Nicole Goosby

BOOKS BY LDP'S CEO, CA$H

TRUST IN NO MAN

TRUST IN NO MAN 2

TRUST IN NO MAN 3

BONDED BY BLOOD

SHORTY GOT A THUG

THUGS CRY

THUGS CRY 2

THUGS CRY 3

TRUST NO BITCH

TRUST NO BITCH 2

TRUST NO BITCH 3

TIL MY CASKET DROPS

RESTRAINING ORDER

RESTRAINING ORDER 2

IN LOVE WITH A CONVICT

Coming Soon

BONDED BY BLOOD 2

BOW DOWN TO MY GANGSTA

Ghost

Printed in the USA
CPSIA information can be obtained
at www.ICGtesting.com
CBHW051225200124
3632CB00011B/779